Second Chance at Love

RUNAWAY LOVE
JASMINE CRAIG

A
SECOND CHANCE AT LOVE
BOOK

Second Chance at Love books are published by
The Berkley/Jove Publishing Group
200 Madison Avenue, New York, NY 10016

- 1 -

"KATE, WHERE ARE YOU? Will you come here, please?"

Kate heard her mother's voice calling from the master bedroom, but she made no reply, and her expression was anxious as she glanced around the kitchen. Her gaze fell on the car keys hanging on a hook by the rear door of the apartment. With an abrupt movement, she snatched the keys, her fingers closing around them convulsively.

She bit her lip as she peeked out into the hallway. It was still deserted. Her father had been talking on the telephone and probably hadn't even noticed that she'd left the living room. He was making a call to one of his employees and nothing less than an earthquake was likely to attract his attention.

"Kate, come here!" her mother called again. "I've finished packing your suitcase, so you can come home with

1

us for a few weeks. There's no reason to stay here in Milwaukee!"

Kate closed the door between the kitchen and the hallway as softly as she could. Any minute they would discover her in the kitchen and the whole, useless argument about her future would start up again. She simply couldn't face another minute of her mother's well-meaning nagging.

With a panic-stricken tug, Kate pulled open the rear service door and slipped out of the apartment. She ran down the back stairs, not waiting for the elevator. Her high-heeled shoes made a sharp staccato on the bare concrete steps. By the time she reached the basement garage, she was panting, her heart pounding as though she had escaped from acute physical danger.

"Hi, Mrs. Danbury! You want your car?" George, the parking attendant, greeted her with a friendly grin. He had been especially courteous these past few weeks since Steven's death. Kate guessed he felt sorry for her because she was a widow and still so young.

"Thanks, but I'll get the car, George. It's in an easy spot to take out." She tried to speak calmly so that he wouldn't ask any awkward questions. She wanted to get away before her parents came rushing to find her. She needed to be by herself for a little while. Since Steven had died, it seemed that her parents hadn't allowed her the luxury of a moment alone. This afternoon had been the final straw when her mother started to make none-too-subtle hints about Kate's need to "get back into the swing of things." Kate wondered which man her mother had lined up for her this time. Earle Darrin, perhaps, or Scott Ballard.

She unlocked the door of the blue Porsche and slid inside, sinking back against the dark upholstery. She grabbed the steering wheel to steady her shaking hands.

"'Bye, George!" She waved her hand as casually as she could. "See you in a little while."

Kate drove out of the city in the gathering darkness, her mind roaming restlessly over the wasteland of her marriage.

Steven's family and her own were two of the most influential in Wisconsin. Everybody had been delighted when handsome Steven Danbury had married beautiful Kate Forsberg, thus uniting two major commercial dynasties. Only Steven and Kate had failed to share in the general rejoicing, pushed into a marriage neither of them particularly wanted by the combined force of two sets of domineering parents.

She'd been only twenty-one, Kate excused herself, wondering how she had ever agreed to make such a disastrous marriage. She was an only child, and her parents had trained her to accept their wishes without question or argument. Kate's father was an energetic, successful businessman whose view of the world was starkly black and white. When she was very young, Kate had learned to conceal from him the fact that her world seemed to be painted entirely in shades of silver-gray.

Having married Steven, it was second nature for Kate to lie about the success of her marriage. Other women, differently brought up, would have filed for divorce. Instead, Kate threw herself into her work, so that the outside world never guessed how bitterly she regretted marrying Steven. He was a spoiled, willful child masquerading in a handsome man's body, and she was compelled to watch him pursue a life that totally excluded her. Steven won friends, as he had won Kate, with a mask of careless charm that he discarded as soon as he stepped into their elegant lakefront apartment in Milwaukee.

For the last two years he hadn't entered their apartment very often. When he died in the hotel fire, he had been away from home "on business" for over three months.

Worst of all, he hadn't been alone when he died. Kate's parents had done their best to keep the truth from her. Even today, nearly two months after Steven's death, they had tried to lie.

"Kate, darling," her mother had protested when Kate plucked up courage to tell her parents that she knew the truth, "you mustn't believe those vicious rumors that the newspapers print. You know how the media loves to spread gossip about the Danburys and the Forsbergs. That's the price we pay for controlling such large corporations."

"But it wasn't gossip," Kate replied quietly. *"You* know that and so do I. The coroner's report said Steven died of smoke inhalation. There was a woman in bed with him, and she died of smoke inhalation, too. They had high alcohol contents in their blood, which is probably why they didn't hear the fire alarms. Almost everybody else in the hotel got out safely, as you know."

A flash of lightning jolted Kate into a sudden awareness of her surroundings. She had driven without thinking of where she was going, wanting only to escape from the smothering attentions of her parents. Now the heavy evening heat had broken in a ferocious thunderstorm, and, as she peered through the rain-blurred windshield, she realized she was lost. She must have turned off Route 41 some time ago because she was driving along a narrow, unnumbered country road. Another flash of lightning illuminated a faded sign that read *Wanpoint*. It might as well have indicated the jungles of Africa for all the significance the name had for Kate.

The fierceness of the storm began to frighten her. She realized how distraught she had been when she'd run out of the apartment. She must be crazy to drive through a thunderstorm on back country roads without knowing how she got where she was. She had only wanted to have thirty minutes' respite from her parents' nagging; she hadn't intended to run away from Milwaukee. Worst of all, in her headlong flight, she hadn't stopped to pick up a purse; she had no money, no credit cards, and no identification.

As if to underline the precariousness of her position, a light glowed on the Porsche's instrument panel, warning her that she'd soon run out of gas. Kate felt alarm feather down her spine as she wondered how she was going to get home.

Utterly deserted, the road gleamed with a sheen of water. The wheels of her car skittered every time she slowed down to search for a sign indicating the entrance to a major highway. Despite the distorting rain, Kate could see that the quality of the road surface had been deteriorating steadily, but she was afraid to admit that the chances of finding an interstate highway were becoming increasingly remote. She drove on doggedly for another ten minutes before the road ended in a forked junction, with no sign to indicate which fork led where.

"Hell!" Kate muttered under her breath. "What do I do now?" With a weary shrug of her shoulders, she took the right-hand fork.

Almost at once, she knew the decision had been a bad one. Within half a mile, the blacktop surface of the road disappeared, to be replaced by a narrow track of bumpy gravel. Treacherous pools of water hid deep potholes. It was pitch-black, so it would only be a matter of time before one of the car's wheels bounced into a muddy hole and stuck there. Kate couldn't risk turning around, however, because she would almost certainly land in one of the water-filled ditches.

Gritting her teeth, she decided to go as far as she could along the narrow track. It had to go somewhere, she reasoned. Her optimism was soon justified when a weather-beaten sign appeared in the glow of her headlights: *Windhaven Farm*.

The fright that had been clutching at her stomach for the last half hour lessened somewhat. A farm! Probably a dairy farm in this part of the state. She imagined a plump, friendly farmer's wife who would willingly provide her with hot coffee and a warm shower. She could explain why she didn't have any money . . . arrange for a transfer of funds to a local bank . . . At that moment the Porsche gave a splutter and the engine died abruptly, jerking her forward against the steering wheel.

For a moment Kate was too dazed to move, then, hesitantly, she pushed open the car door and stepped out into the lashing rain. Within a minute she was drenched. With a feeling of relief she saw the outline of the farmhouse in the distance and ran toward it. Water squelched inside her shoes and her breath came in hard, short gasps. Her hair was plastered into a dark golden mass around her face, and her silk dress clung to her body, outlining every slender curve.

She almost fell against the front door of the farmhouse and beat on the wooden panels with her knuckles. No one came. Kate pounded on the door again. There are lights inside, she told herself, forcing down her fear. Somebody must be home.

The door opened so suddenly that she lost her balance and fell forward, clutching at the arm of the tall, dark man who stood there.

He cast one quick, all-embracing glance over her, then moved to shut the door. "Go away," he said. "You can tell Sacha I'm not coming back."

Too bewildered to reply, Kate continued to lean weakly against him. Anybody less like the plump and friendly farmer's wife of her imagination would have been hard to find. His hard muscles pressed against her body and his lean, sinewy strength was emphasized by the black sweater and tight, faded jeans he wore. His black hair slashed in a careless line across his forehead and, in the dim light of the hallway, his skin looked sallow under its tan, as if he had once spent a great deal of time outdoors but hadn't done so in a while. His eyes were dark with hostility and his tense body projected a latent anger that was reinforced by the rigid line of his mouth. Kate looked at him and shivered.

With a gesture almost of contempt, he pulled his hand away from her clutching fingers. "Where's your car?" he asked. "I'll see you off my property."

"It's down there. Down the path." Her teeth were starting to chatter with the combined effects of cold and shock. "I'm out of gas," she said. "The car won't go."

He gave a harsh laugh, totally devoid of amusement. "How devastatingly unoriginal. Surely Sacha could suggest a better excuse than that?"

"Who is Sacha? I don't know anybody called Sacha." She pressed her hand to her forehead, trying to still the throbbing in her temples.

Something in the weariness of her voice caused his expression to soften a little. Abruptly he dragged her inside the house and thrust her under the single, unshaded light bulb, turning up her face to examine it more closely. "You look half-drowned," he said brusquely. "What happened? Did you lose your way trying to find my house? How the hell did Sacha find out I was in Wisconsin, anyway?"

She was terrified by the strength of his hands as they gripped her shoulders, forcing her to remain motionless under the glare of the light. "I was lost," she said and her body started to shake convulsively. "Please let me go now. I'll s-sleep in the c-car. I won't trouble you any more."

He released her as abruptly as he had seized her, and studied her intently. His expression changed from anger to indifference. "You can stay for the night if you want. God knows, the house is big enough for two people." He turned away from her, not bothering to observe her reaction to his grudging invitation. "There are clean towels and sheets in the linen closet upstairs. There's a bathroom, second door on your right. The spare bedroom is next to the bathroom."

He made no effort to see how she felt about his curt directions. A gust of wind slammed the front door shut behind Kate. The man shrugged almost imperceptibly, as if the wind had decided her fate and now she was certain to stay. He walked into a nearby room and closed the door. Distractedly, Kate noticed that he dragged his left foot slightly as he moved.

She stood in the bleak hallway, shivering as much with fright as with cold. Her dress was dripping water onto the bare stone floor and droplets of rain trickled from her hair down between her breasts. She wondered why, with all the farmhouses in Wisconsin, she had to choose one inhabited by a madman. The noise of the storm died away temporarily, and Kate found herself straining to hear some sound from behind the door to the room the man had entered. There was nothing, only an impenetrable silence. She shook herself out of the lethargy she knew was induced by hunger and thirst as much as by fatigue. She hadn't been eating enough recently, she knew.

Despite her exhaustion, common sense told her that she couldn't stay there. It would be safer to sleep in the car, however uncomfortable that alternative seemed at the moment. Kate dragged her feet in the direction of the front door, but the heel on her right sandal was loose, and she twisted her ankle awkwardly as she walked across the damp flagstones.

A sudden brilliant flash of lightning streaked across the sky, followed by a crash of thunder that sounded as though the heavens themselves were about to fall on the roof of the farmhouse. Lightning flashed again and, with an answering flicker, the light went out, leaving the hallway in total darkness.

The muffling blackness was the last straw for Kate. She screamed with all the force of twenty-four hours of accumulated frustration. She screamed again, and once she had started she didn't seem able to stop. She heard a door flung open and a muttered curse as the man stumbled over a piece of furniture in the darkness.

"Why the hell are you screaming?" She felt his hands close around her waist, producing a sudden shaft of sensation so powerful that it frightened her.

"Let me go!" She pulled herself out of his grasp and ran blindly away, no longer caring about the impenetrable blackness.

She was aware of one sharp moment of agonizing pain as her head struck something solid, and then there was only darkness.

- 2 -

WHEN KATE REGAINED consciousness, the ache in her head was so intense that it momentarily blotted out all other sensations. Slowly, she became aware that she was in bed, and she ran her fingers over the smooth cotton sheets before looking up at the man seated beside her. As far as she knew, he was a complete stranger. She wondered why he was staring at her, his dark eyes hard with dislike.

"How are you feeling?" he asked curtly.

"My head aches. . . . Who are you? Why am I here?"

The man frowned, his gaze watchful as he scrutinized her pale features.

"There was a power failure and you banged your head. You've been unconscious for quite a while."

"I don't remember why I'm here," she said and her forehead wrinkled in a mixture of pain and frustration. "Who are you? I'm Kate . . . I'm Kate . . ." Her voice faded away. "I can't remember my other name," she whispered and the panic she felt must have shown in her eyes, for the man put out his hand to stop her restless clutching at the sheet.

"Don't you remember who sent you here?" he asked. "Don't you remember Sacha? You're probably an actress. . . Maybe a model?"

"I don't know anybody called Sacha." The panic was more acute now, making her feel faintly sick. An elusive memory tugged at the corner of her mind, making her head ache. "I'm running away. . . . "

His mouth twisted wryly. "Aren't we all?"

She reached out and tugged at his arm, seeking the reassurance and comfort he seemed reluctant to give. "Please help me. . . . I can't remember anything."

He shook her hand away and got up from the bed. She could almost feel his anger. "Don't push your luck, baby. Is this your cute way of getting an invitation to stay? If it weren't for the bump on the side of your head, I'd be wondering if you hadn't staged the whole accident. Are you *sure* you don't remember who you are?"

"You're crazy," she said bitterly. "Why should I pretend to lose my memory? What's the possible advantage of that?" The pain in her head was swelling until it was impossible to think, and she dashed away the tears shining in her green eyes. "I don't want to stay here. I want to go home." Even as she spoke, she felt a wrenching conviction that she was lying. She didn't want to go home, wherever that was. The realization made her feel even more sick.

The man pushed her back against the pillow. His movements became more gentle, although she could still sense the antagonism hovering beneath his superficial calm. "You'd better rest," he said abruptly. "Here, drink this."

Her distrust must have been plain to see, for he lifted the glass to his own lips and swallowed about a quarter of the contents. "It's lemon juice, sugar, and liquid pain killer," he said. "What the hell did you think it was? What do you imagine I'm planning to do? Murder you? Rape you while you're unconscious? Believe me, you're safe. I don't enjoy taking skinny neurotics into my bed. I prefer a little warmth and friendly cooperation."

She took the glass from him, knowing that her cheeks were dark with an embarrassed flush. "I'm scared," she said. "Can't you imagine what it's like not to remember who you are, or what you've done?"

He drew in his breath sharply. "It sounds like heaven to me." He seemed to regret having spoken, for he moved away from the bed almost at once and blew out the candle which he'd placed on the night table. He made his way to the door with the aid of a pocket flashlight.

"I'm going to see about switching the electric power over to the emergency generator. Get some rest. You'll feel better in the morning. I expect you'll remember everything after a good night's sleep."

Kate wished she could share his confidence. She closed her eyes anyway because the ache in her head was less severe that way. She was asleep before he had time to close the door.

It was morning when she awoke for the second time. She tried to sit, but was overcome by a wave of nausea and collapsed against the pillow just as the man walked into her room. She noticed again the slight, almost imperceptible, limp.

This morning he wore a white shirt tucked into his jeans, the buttons left casually unfastened almost to his waist. She felt her gaze drawn to the strong, brown column of his throat and noticed the dark hair that grew on his chest, disappearing at the low-slung waistline of his jeans. She looked away at once, but was aware of a sudden increase in the throbbing of her pulse. She couldn't understand her reaction. Steven had told her over and over again that she was the next best thing to frigid. He'd said that making love to her was like making love to a block of ice that wouldn't melt.

Kate felt the blood drain from her face. She remembered who she was! She was Kate Danbury...and she wished she wasn't. She turned her face away from the man, trying to avoid the sharp scrutiny of his dark eyes.

"I've brought you something to eat, Kate." His voice was still cool, but it bore none of the harsh overtones of the previous night. "Are you hungry? You missed dinner yesterday."

She guessed that his seemingly casual words were a subtle probe to help him find out if her memory had returned. She knew she ought to reassure him. She ought to say: Hi, I'm Kate Danbury and I have to get back to my parents. She opened her mouth to speak, but no words came out. The thought of picking up the threads of her old life made her stomach contract with fear, and the fear showed in her eyes.

He came and stood by the bed, arranging the tray across her lap. "Lost your tongue?" he asked and his voice was guarded. "How do you feel this morning?"

She realized he had again misinterpreted that flash of panic in her eyes. He thought her memory was still a blank. She allowed her long, thick lashes to drop over her eyes, hiding her expression. She could hardly believe she had actually decided to deceive this man. "My headache's better," she said huskily.

He cupped her chin in his hands, forcing her to look at him. "What is it, Kate? What's troubling you?"

"I can't remember my other name," she said and her voice shook with the telling of the lie. "I don't know why I'm here. Who are you?"

For a moment she thought he wasn't going to believe her. She felt the coldness of his scrutiny before his features relaxed once again. "There was a storm," he said matter-of-factly. "You banged your head on the kitchen door when the lights went out." After a brief pause, he added, "I suspect your memory will come back if you rest for a while. I think the concussion has gone."

"What is this place? What am I doing here?"

He laughed without humor. "I was hoping you could tell me why you're here."

"Why are you . . . angry with me? What have I done?"

"I'm not angry with you," he said curtly. "I'm mad as hell at Sacha."

"Who's Sacha?"

There was a short pause before he answered her. "Let's forget about Sacha for a while. The bathroom's next door. Can you get dressed and make it down to the kitchen for breakfast after you've eaten that snack? You need something more substantial."

For the first time she gave some thought to her appearance and realized she was wearing nothing except a man's shirt. A wave of color darkened her body from toes to scalp. It was disturbing to think of this man undressing her. "I can't get dressed," she said, looking at the torn shreds of gray silk that hung over the chair. "My dress is ruined and I don't have anything else to wear."

"What about the blue suitcase in your car?"

She threw him a puzzled glance. "There isn't a blue suitcase in my car. I didn't bring a suitcase."

He was at her side in an instant, his hands pinning her to the bed, his expression menacing. "Isn't it strange, Kate, that you remember you don't have a suitcase but forget part of your own name?"

She was scared by the ease with which he had trapped her. "I don't know what you mean. I haven't forgotten everything. I can remember some things . . . like last night, for instance." She twisted her head again so that she wouldn't have to meet his angry gaze. "I can remember driving through the storm and I know I got lost," she added.

His hands tightened around her wrists. "If I thought you were lying to me, Kate my sweet, I'd make sure you went back to Sacha with a story worth telling."

"I don't know anybody called Sacha. Please, I'm telling you the truth."

He continued to look at her for several minutes and she forced herself to remain impassive under his inspection. At last he stood up. "I'll bring you some clothes. By the way, my name's Blake . . . just in case you didn't know already." He left the room without another word.

There was some juice and a sweet roll on the tray he had brought up for her. She didn't feel hungry, but she made herself finish everything. She hadn't eaten in twenty-four hours. She swayed when she got out of bed, but she felt better after she had taken a shower. Her headache was almost gone. There was a new toothbrush, still wrapped in cellophane, resting at one side of the old-fashioned sink, as well as a comb and fresh towels. She wondered why the man . . . Blake . . . was so thoughtful in certain matters and so irrationally angry in others.

She examined her surroundings carefully as she combed out the tangles in her long hair. If she concentrated on practicalities, she wouldn't have to ask herself why she was continuing with this crazy pretense of amnesia. The bathroom was tiled in a hideous shade of maroon that might have been fashionable in the late nineteen forties and the cracked linoleum on the floor was a dingy checkerboard of gray and white. It was a strange place to find a man like Blake. Something about the inherent arrogance of his bearing made her think that he had once lived in very different surroundings.

When she went back into the bedroom, she found a gingham blouse and a denim wrap-around skirt laid out on the bed. A pair of sturdy canvas shoes, still in a box and obviously never worn, rested on the rag rug at the side of the bed. She dressed quickly, suddenly anxious to get downstairs and start the day.

Blake was pouring himself a mug of coffee when she walked into the kitchen, and the smell of warm toast made her feel hungry. She pushed the heavy weight of hair away from the nape of her neck, and Blake's expression tightened. "The clothes fit you well," he said shortly.

"Yes." She hesitated on the threshold of the kitchen. "Thank you. I was expecting a pair of your cast-off jeans and a too-big shirt."

"Come and sit down." He didn't explain where he had found the feminine clothing. "Would you like some coffee? Toast? Cereal?"

"I'm so hungry this morning. It must be the country air."

"You live in the city?"

She wasn't going to fall into another trap. "I don't know.... I don't remember."

His mouth tightened into a grim line, but he pushed the percolator toward her without comment. "Help yourself to coffee. There's honey and jam already on the table."

She had forgotten how delicious food could taste. In the weeks since Steven's death she had only eaten when the housekeeper actually put food in front of her and everything had tasted like sawdust.

"That was fantastic," she said when she had finished the last morsel.

"Have some more," he replied, and she thought she could detect the first faint note of amusement in his voice. "I daresay we have another slice of bread somewhere."

She actually laughed aloud. My God, how many months had it been since she last laughed aloud? "I was starving. I'm sorry if I've eaten all of your breakfast supplies."

"Exactly how long is it since you last ate a square meal?" he asked casually, too casually.

The laughter vanished from her eyes. "I don't know. A long time, I think. I'll stack these plates in the dishwasher, if you want."

"This house doesn't have a dishwasher."

"I guess I could wash them in the sink. My hands still function, even if my memory's gone." She gathered up the mugs and plates and carried them to the sink.

Blake watched her in silence for a moment before he spoke. "As soon as you've done the dishes, I'll drive you to the local hospital and check you in."

The mug she was washing dropped into the old-fashioned plastic bowl, disappearing beneath the detergent bubbles. "I don't want to go to hospital! I'm not sick! Why can't I stay here?"

He shrugged, apparently immune to her pleas. "You can't remember who you are or why you're here. I've checked the car. There's no identification in it and no luggage of any sort. That's pretty unusual. If you have amnesia, as you claim, you need professional help. If you don't have amnesia, I don't want you here. Either way, you have to go."

"But I don't want to go! Please . . . don't make me leave here."

"Amnesia is a serious medical disorder. It shouldn't be treated lightly."

She wondered if there was any way she could persuade Blake to let her remain hidden for a few days. It felt so wonderful to be with somebody who knew her only as Kate: a woman in her own right. Not the daughter of the multimillionaire Forsbergs, or the socialite wife of Steven Danbury. Just Kate. It was exhilarating to think that with Blake she could pretend to be whoever she wanted to be. She glanced at him, only half aware of the veiled invitation that she let shine in her green eyes. "If I could stay here, I think I would get better soon. It's very peaceful. . . ."

"Sure, that's a great idea. And as soon as Sacha arrives, I daresay you'll stage a miraculous recovery. What were your instructions, I wonder? To soften me up and keep my bed warm at night so I wouldn't get restless and move on? Were you supposed to calm me down and make me more willing to listen to Sacha's lies? After all, everybody knows I have a weakness for green-eyed blondes. The only mystery is why Sacha didn't come himself, except that maybe—for once—he realized he'd overplayed his hand. Do you know what Sacha said to me before I left Fiji? 'Forget about Kevin,' he said. Forget! Of course, Kevin's dead and, as far as Sacha's concerned, that's the end of it. What the hell does it matter if Kevin was my friend?"

"I don't know what you're shouting about. I keep telling you I don't know Sacha, or Kevin . . . or anybody."

"I hope you act better than you lie, sweetie. Otherwise you'll never make it off the casting couch and onto the screen. Hasn't anybody ever told you it's a jungle out there? Directors like Sacha eat little girls like you before breakfast, and, believe me, they don't suffer from indigestion afterwards."

"I told you the truth when I arrived here last night. I lost my way."

"Sure, honey. And you went for a drive in the middle of the year's worst thunderstorm because you like seeing Wisconsin scenery in the rain. All that wet grass really turns you on."

"Okay!" She shouted the word, her eyes flashing with anger and her stomach churning with the sharpness of her inexplicable sense of loss. "All right! So take me to the hospital emergency room. I don't care!" She flung down the dish towel she was clutching and stormed over to the kitchen door. She would have to explain to the doctors what had happened and ask them to contact her parents. It had been such a brief taste of freedom. . . . But she wasn't going to confess to Blake that she had been lying, that she remembered only too well who she was: dull, boring Kate Danbury, who couldn't keep her husband faithful even through three years of marriage.

"Can you cook?"

His mild question was so unexpected that she didn't stop to consider her answer. "Well, yes. Of course."

"How do you know?"

"There are some things I just know."

"And do you *just know* if you're a good housekeeper? Could you clean this place up a little?"

"I guess so."

"If you're prepared to work for your keep, you can stay until the weekend. If your memory hasn't come back by then, I'm taking you to the local hospital. Don't try the misty-eyes-sparkling-with-tears routine on me twice." Almost to himself, he added, "I must be out of my own mind to consider letting you stay."

She ignored his muttered comment. "Oh, thank you, Blake! I'll work hard. You won't regret your decision, I promise."

"Won't I?"

She was careful to show no reaction to the self-mockery in his voice. "Which room would you like me to clean first?"

He shrugged. "The living room seems an obvious choice, but the whole house could use a thorough cleaning." He watched her through narrowed eyes. "Isn't there somebody at home who'll be worrying about where you are?"

Quickly she dropped her lashes to conceal the flash of guilty knowledge in her eyes. She knew she ought to let her parents know where she was. "I don't remember," she said after a long pause. "I don't feel as if anybody is worrying about me."

"What about your husband?"

"My husband's d—" Hastily she altered the words into a question. "My husband? I don't think I'm married."

He sighed. "Forget it, Kate. We'll play it your way, but you really are a rotten liar. Why are you wearing a wedding ring if you're not married?"

She smothered a gasp as she looked down at the wide platinum band circling the third finger of her left hand. There was no way she could pretend it was merely a decorative piece of jewelry.

He cut off her garbled attempt at an explanation before she had stumbled through the first few words. "I said forget it, Kate. I'll see you at dinnertime. Let's skip lunch, shall we? It's already nearly noon."

"All right." She kept her burning cheeks averted. "I'll be happy to cook an early dinner. Does five o'clock sound good?"

"Sounds fine." He walked out of the kitchen, leaving

Kate to search for cleaning supplies in the cabinet under the sink.

It took her three hours to clean the living room, and when it was all finished she had to admit it was still a shabby room, with no claim to elegance. But it smelled of fresh polish and the windows sparkled in the sun, highlighting the flower vases she had filled with half-wild marigolds. Kate carried her cleaning supplies back to the kitchen, humming under her breath.

She found some teabags in one of the cabinets and brewed a batch of iced tea. She went outside, carrying the plastic jug. As far as she could see in any direction there was nothing but green fields, trees, blue sky, and sun. The only signs of human construction, outside the yard itself, were the fences that broke up the stretches of lush grass and the tall poles carrying power cables. A low-flying, single-engine plane broke the peacefulness of the empty countryside, reminding her that civilization was probably not many miles away. She watched the plane until it was a mere speck on the horizon, reveling in the feel of the hot sun on her shoulders, then she turned and made her way down to the barn. Blake was working at the top of a ladder, a sheen of sweat on the darkly-tanned skin of his naked back.

He stopped working when he heard her approach, sliding down the ladder incredibly fast and jumping off lightly a few rungs from the bottom. Kate saw the brief moment of pain register on his face as his left leg took the weight of his jump. He immediately controlled his features to obliterate the signs of pain and wiped his hands on his discarded shirt before reaching out to take the jug of tea from her. She smelled the sharp tang of his body's heat and felt a pulse start to hammer at the base of her throat.

"I brought some iced tea," she said, as if he couldn't see perfectly well what she was carrying.

"A gift from heaven. Painting's thirsty work in this heat."

"At least the humidity's gone. The storm last night

cleared the air." It wasn't very scintillating conversation, but she was out of practice as far as making idle chitchat was concerned.

There was a slight pause before Blake answered her. "Yes. Last night's storm blew away a great many cobwebs. How's the housecleaning going?"

"Pretty well, but there's about three inches of dust over everything. Have you been living here long?"

There was another pause. "My mother died last October, so the house was empty. She sold the stock when my father died, five years ago."

"I'm sorry." She noticed that he hadn't actually answered her question, and she was curious to find out something about him. "Were you living somewhere else before your mother died?"

"Yes. I've led a pretty wandering existence, so far." Abruptly he handed her the jug of tea and his empty glass. "Thanks for the drink." He walked back to the ladder, indicating that the conversation was over. "See you for dinner at five," he said, returning to his painting.

She walked slowly toward the farmhouse, thinking about Blake, and wondering why he was so reticent about his personal life. A wry smile twisted her mouth when she realized what she was thinking. In the circumstances, she could hardly complain about people who wanted to keep their pasts private. Wasn't she involved in a deliberate deception simply because she found the last three years too painful to even think about?

Kate dumped the jug and glasses into the sink with a decided clatter, not very pleased with the trend of her thoughts. She set about scrubbing the kitchen with methodical thoroughness, not caring that she ruined her perfectly manicured nails. One of the good things about hard physical work, she decided later, was that it didn't leave much energy to spare for useless speculation. She had had altogether too much time to brood in the past few weeks.

By the time the kitchen was cleaned to her satisfaction,

it was time to start preparing dinner. She removed two steaks and a package of frozen mushrooms from the old-fashioned freezer chest she found standing on the back porch. She was relieved to see that it was quite well stocked. At least Blake wasn't so hard up that he couldn't afford to eat properly. She found some mocha ice cream they could have for dessert. It wasn't going to be a gourmet meal, but anything would taste good after the physically active day they had both spent.

She took a shower and was waiting in the living room when Blake finally joined her. He had showered, too, and his hair gleamed raven-black in the light of the early evening sun. The faint pallor she had noticed beneath his tan had already started to disappear. He had changed into a pair of casual cords and a loose-knit shirt, faded from frequent washings. Irrationally, she found herself wishing she had something more glamorous to wear than a denim skirt and a dust-streaked gingham shirt. It was faintly annoying that Blake should seem so impervious to her feminine charms.

In fact, he scarcely gave her a second glance. He put down the heavy tray he was carrying and walked across the room to peer out of the clean windows. "The house looks great," he said. He saw the bowls of wild flowers on the window ledges and his harsh features relaxed into a cynical smile. "Have you decided the house needs a few feminine touches, Kate?"

Her heart raced a little faster as the warmth of his smile touched her. Despite his cynicism, Blake could exercise a potent attraction when he wanted to. Deliberately, she turned her gaze away from his smile. She wasn't going to involve herself for a second time with a man whose moods alternated between moments of charm and hours of inexplicable brooding. Steven had taught her more than she wanted to know about men who traded on their superficial sex appeal and then had nothing more to offer. She managed to keep her voice absolutely cool.

"I'm glad you like the changes because I want to earn

my keep. I prefer never to be in debt."

He didn't bother to conceal his amusement. "Very commendable sentiments, my dear, but it's a pity about your eyes. Didn't they talk to you about your eyes in drama school? It's difficult to look full of Puritan virtue when your eyes are misty with the promise of passion. It's bad technique to muddle your signals, Kate. The mark of an amateur."

"I think my eyes must be misleading you," she said as formally as she could. "Perhaps I'm starting a bout of hay fever. That would explain any misty expression."

To her surprise, Blake laughed. He opened one of the bottles of beer he had carried in and handed her a tall, chilled glass. "I hope you drink beer. There's nothing else alcoholic in the house."

She smiled. "How can you ask that question in Wisconsin of all places? Of course beer is fine." She sipped the icy cold lager, strangely exhilarated by their conversation. "Dinner can be ready as soon as I broil the steaks," she said.

"I'm hungry, so let's cook them right away. We can eat in the kitchen." His voice was friendly, and he moved quickly to catch her hand, preventing her from leaving the living room. "Truce, Kate?" he asked. "You did a great job with the house and I appreciate it." This time, the smile he gave her held not the smallest trace of mockery.

"Truce," she agreed, and tried not to wonder whether she was relieved or sorry when he dropped her hand and walked briskly into the kitchen.

- 3 -

BLAKE MADE HER laugh all through the meal, entertaining her with stories about the first camping trip he had ever taken with his parents. He made every story come alive for her, so that she seemed to see the hard-working man who had been his father as well as the small, mischievous boy Blake once had been. At one point in the story he even appeared to become a hungry old bear, sniffing around the camp supplies, although Kate secretly thought that that part of the story might have been invented purely for her entertainment. She couldn't remember when she had last enjoyed a meal so much.

She made coffee when they had finished eating and, by mutual consent, they carried their cups out to the screened porch, sitting in the sagging wicker chairs to watch the sun dip down behind the tree-lined horizon. Kate felt replete and pleasantly sleepy. She wondered how Blake guessed that she no longer felt in the mood to chatter. They watched the evening darken into night in an unbroken but companionable silence. For the first time in months, Kate realized that she was hovering on the edge of total relaxation. Strange, she thought, stealing a covert glance at Blake, how one part of her could feel so relaxed when another part of her seemed to tremble on the brink of some exciting new discovery.

Her meandering thoughts were shattered by an insistent banging on the front door. Blake was on his feet in a second, dragging her up and swinging her around to face him. His anger was all the more shocking because it contrasted so violently with the harmony they had just shared.

"So you found the telephone in my bedroom," he said, and his eyes glittered with a bitter accusation. He gave a harsh laugh. "My God! After all those years in Hollywood, I was still crazy enough to think you might be the one woman who could be trusted. Take care of those green eyes of yours, Kate. They're quite a weapon."

She struggled to get out of his arms, but he held her effortlessly, not even needing two hands. "Let me go!" she commanded angrily. "I don't understand what your obsession is all about, Blake, and frankly I don't care. Who am I supposed to have telephoned? Sacha? I've told you a hundred times that I've never met anybody called Sacha."

He laughed derisively. "How would you know, honey? You've lost your memory, remember? Have you forgotten that you're supposed to have amnesia?"

She wriggled out of his grip at last. "I agree with just one thing you've said, Blake. You're crazy."

The banging at the front door became even louder, and Blake caught her wrist again, dragging her through the living room and into the hall. "Don't think you're running off somewhere," he said. "You're not escaping from this little episode scot-free. I hope Sacha's paid you in advance, or you'll never see a cent of what he promised you. I'll make sure of that."

He pulled open the front door, and he was holding Kate so close to his side that she felt his shock. Her own body froze into an icy statue. She actually clutched Blake's arm for support. "Mother!" she said hoarsely. "Dad! However did you find me here?"

Her mother swept the dingy hallway with one glance. As usual, she ignored her daughter's question.

"Oh, Kate, how could you! Leaving us without a word when you knew your father needed to get those papers signed right away!"

Before Kate could begin to find a suitable reply, her parents marched into the house. Her mother was careful not to touch the walls, as if she feared either dust or some other form of contamination.

"Please do come in," Blake said ironically and stepped aside so that they could enter the living room. "Feel right at home."

Kate had to stifle a faintly hysterical giggle, but she should have guessed that Blake's sarcasm would be entirely wasted on her parents, who were already three quarters of the way into the living room.

"I thought you had more sense, Kate," her mother said as she looked disparagingly around the shabby room. "Haven't you got a grain of practicality?"

"I think I have." Kate sighed wearily. She wondered why she always felt exhausted as soon as her parents were anywhere near her. "How did you find me?" she asked for the second time.

"Private investigators, of course," snapped her father. "We were afraid you'd crashed somewhere in the back-woods. I ordered two planes to fly out of Milwaukee on a hundred-mile radius. We could scarcely believe it when the agency reported that their plane had spotted a pale blue Porsche parked in the driveway of some rundown farmhouse fifty miles from Milwaukee! And when they ran a quick check on the farm's owner and found out what he did . . ." As if recollecting that he was a guest in the house he was complaining about, her father bit off his remaining words.

"Would you like a beer?" Blake asked politely. Kate had the incredible impression that he was actually laughing to himself. She couldn't understand it. Nobody ever laughed at her father, particularly when he lost his temper.

"We don't have time, thanks." Her father checked his watch in the same reflex gesture he always used when cutting short an inconvenient business meeting. "We only came to talk some reason into Kate here." He looked at his daughter, his expression a bewildered mixture of pain and annoyance. "I told you *twice* last week that I needed you to come over to my office and sign some papers, Kate. How could you take off like that?" Almost as an afterthought, he added, "Your mother was sick with worry. Anything might have happened to you, driving in the state you were in."

Kate stared fixedly at her hand, surprised to find that it still clutched Blake's arm. She was even more surprised to find that she had no desire to move it. She was afraid it might give her parents the wrong idea if they saw her grasping Blake for support, but at the moment she felt she needed to borrow some of his strength. She cleared her throat nervously. "I'm . . . er . . . not signing any more papers for you, Dad. I have a consultant to advise me on all my financial affairs now. I already told you that."

"A woman banker! For God's sake, Kate, what does she know? You don't expect me to take that appointment seriously, do you? I can't believe Steven was so careless as to leave the estate to you, without naming me as trustee."

Kate wouldn't look at her father. "I've given the job to Ms. Bergdorf, Dad, and I'm not changing my mind. She's the sole trustee for my inheritance."

Her mother jumped up from the chair. "I don't know what's gotten into you recently, I really don't. You knew your father wanted to appoint himself and Earle Darrin as joint trustees. Earle is just the right man for the job. And what do you suppose Earle's family is going to think when they find out you've been spending time with some out-of-work movie stuntman? And only a month or so after Steven..."

Kate's voice was dangerously quiet when she interrupted her mother. "What has Earle's family got to do with where I choose to spend my time?"

"You know Earle is the ideal man for you to marry, Kate," her father replied impatiently, "so you don't want to offend his family. His brother is studying to be a minister, you know, and they set very high moral standards. Earle's father and I are planning to merge our lumber interests in the northern part of the state, but, apart from that, he's the perfect choice for your next husband. His parents sent him to a prep school out East to be educated, just like your mother sent you, and he's always going to art galleries and concerts. His father told me just the other day that Earle's planning a state-wide art auction to be held in the fall. Now, isn't that the sort of thing you like to take part in? You know you like him, Kate, and you need a man to look after you."

"No, I don't. I can look after myself if I'm allowed to. What you really mean is that you want to control the man who marries me, so that you can take charge of my inheritance."

"Well, you certainly aren't capable of taking charge of it yourself! Do you think I haven't heard rumors about what you're planning to do? Wake up to reality, Kate! It's time to stop fooling around with charitable foundations and come home with us. We pay enough taxes to the government already. Let them pay for another damnfool education center for handicapped children."

An involuntary shudder rippled down Kate's spine, but before she could speak, Blake draped an arm casually around her shoulders and pulled her tightly against his side. She looked up at him in surprise, although she felt no urge to move out of his grasp.

"Well, now," Blake said with a slow drawl, gazing steadily at Kate's father. "I don't think you've understood the situation here. Kate and I are planning to get married, you know."

"What!" Her mother and father shouted the word in unison.

Kate's mouth fell open. "M-married?" she stuttered. "You and m-me?"

His arm tightened fractionally, warning her. "Now, honey, you know how long we've been talking about this. There's no need to be shy in front of your parents. They had to find out about us some time or another."

Her mouth continued to hang open. Blake took care of her all-too-apparent astonishment by bending his head and dropping a casual kiss on her parted lips. Her stomach immediately gave an inexplicable lurch, and she snapped her mouth shut. Blake's eyes stared teasingly into hers, their dark brown depths dancing with laughter—and some other emotion she was too startled to try to decipher.

Her father's annoyance exploded into open rage. "Married! Are you out of your mind, Kate? Don't you have any pride? Don't you care that he'll be marrying you for your money?"

"Why do you say that?"

Her father looked relieved that his daughter's question was phrased so calmly. Kate realized he'd never learned that the angrier she felt inside, the more her superficial calm increased.

"Kate, think ahead for once. It didn't take my investigators four hours to come up with a complete rundown on Blake Koehler. He was kicked out of the local high school as a troublemaker, disappeared for six years, and turned up in Hollywood where he earned a living as a movie stuntman. For the last five years he hasn't even managed to do that successfully. Our investigators couldn't turn up a single stunt assignment awarded to Blake Koehler since he worked on a James Bond movie five years ago. For God's sake, is that the sort of man you plan to marry? It's an insult to Steven's memory!"

Kate allowed her anger to show at last. "Do you always judge people by their position in life? Can't you ever see them as human beings instead of employees?"

"And can't you ever take off your rose-colored glasses? This is a man who can't even find work as a stuntman anymore. His name has been dropped from all the agency lists. God knows how you first met him, but you're here in this farmhouse, so you've seen the way he lives. Are you trying to kid yourself that he wants *you?* Don't you realize he's after your money?"

"The Forsberg–Danbury millions. . . . It would never occur to you that I have any attractions to stack up against that, would it?"

"Money has enabled you to live a very comfortable life, Kate," her mother interjected. "Are you pretending you don't want it? It's easy to be scornful about the power of money when you've never had to do without. Ask Blake Koehler what it feels like to be without a cent to your name."

Kate's father nodded his agreement before glancing at his watch again. "I don't have time to argue with her," he muttered under his breath. "She'll soon see how loudly money talks." He looked assessingly in Blake's direction, taking in the faded cord pants and much-washed shirt. "How much will it take?" he asked bluntly. "How much do I have to offer you to stay away from my daughter?" He reached inside his jacket and pulled out a checkbook, unclipping a gold ballpoint pen from the same pocket. "How about five thousand dollars?" he suggested.

Blake's cold smile was hard to interpret. "You're joking, I think."

Mr. Forsberg swore under his breath. "Okay. Five thousand now and a thousand dollars every month for the next year if you stay away from my daughter."

Blake looked at Kate's white cheeks through narrowed eyes. She felt sick with humiliation, wondering what he

must think of this degrading scene. When he turned back
to confront her father, his face was expressionless, all trace
of mirth removed. "What if I told you Kate and I are in
love?"

"Then I'd say you were fools. Love never put a cent into
any man's pocket. Has she told you that most of her capital
reverted to the Danbury family and the rest of it is all tied
up in a trust fund? You'll never spend a penny of her capital,
even if she does agree to marry you. And her annual income
isn't going to keep you in much luxury."

Mr. Forsberg was writing as he spoke, and he added his
signature to the bottom of the check with a flourish. Blake
took the check in silence and examined it with painstaking
thoroughness. Kate held her breath. If he accepted it, she
would throw up.

"Six thousand dollars." Blake read. He laughed, then
ripped the check into a dozen pieces. Kate slumped against
him, weak with relief.

His glance flickered over her, then turned contemp-
tuously to her parents. "I'd say, Mr. Forsberg, that you
undervalue your daughter."

"The only thing I undervalued was the appeal of her
money. If you imagine you'll be able to break the trust,
you'll find out you're wrong." Mr. Forsberg's reply was an
angry snarl. He had given up even the smallest pretense of
normal courtesy toward Blake.

Kate felt her legs start to tremble, but once again Blake
came to her rescue, his arm supporting her with unobtrusive
strength.

Mr. Forsberg stared at them for a moment, his lips
clamped into a tight line of disapproval. "I'm going to the
car." He walked out without saying good-bye.

Mrs. Forsberg smoothed down the folds of her sunray-
pleated dress. Her cheeks were mottled with splotches of
hectic color. "Are you coming with us, Kate?" she asked.

Slowly, silently, Kate shook her head.

Her mother hovered uncertainly in the doorway as if, for

once in her life, she wasn't sure what she should do next. "I don't understand what's gotten into you," she repeated sadly. "We've always tried to do what's best for you, Kate, and this is all the thanks you give us."

"I want to lead my own life, Mother. I'm twenty-five. I'm not a child any more."

"And you think *that* man will let you lead your own life?" Her mother gave a strange, gasping laugh. "Have you looked at him, Kate? I mean really looked at him with your eyes wide open?" She turned away, as if regretting that she had spoken to her daughter without measuring her words more carefully. "Good-bye, Kate. I guess it's going to be a while before we see you again. Just remember your father and I both warned you that you're making a terrible mistake." She closed the door firmly behind her.

It was Blake who broke the silence after the car engine faded into the distance. He was smiling, seemingly quite unperturbed by the scene they had just gone through.

"I owe you an apology, Kate. You really didn't know Sacha. Next time I must try listening when you tell me something."

Kate's answering smile was strained. "I didn't know Sacha. But I didn't have amnesia . . . at least, I only lost my memory for a short while when I first regained consciousness."

"I guessed that. I already told you, Kate, you're a lousy actress." Without quite knowing how she got there, Kate found herself sitting beside him on the shabby living room sofa. "Do you want to tell me about it?" he asked. "How did you end up here last night?"

It was suddenly amazingly easy to tell him the truth. "My husband died just a little while ago. His family organized a special memorial service yesterday. Afterwards, my parents kept nagging me to go home with them. I couldn't bear it. I wanted to be alone, to try to understand what had happened to Steven and me, and I think I panicked. I ran out of my apartment and started driving. By the time

I stopped to ask myself where I was going, I'd lost my way and the car was almost out of gas. It was just a quirk of fate that the car happened to stop at the end of your driveway."

"Fate—" He gave a strange laugh. "I wish all quirks of fate could be so innocent." With a brief gesture, he seemed to pull himself out of his moment of introspection. "You're welcome to stay here for tonight if you want, Kate. Or I'll drive you back to the city if you would prefer it. I'm only sorry I wasn't in the mood to be more understanding last night."

For some reason, she didn't feel able to meet his eyes. His kindness was more difficult to cope with than his previous wary hostility. "I'd prefer to stay here," she said. "I'm not . . . I'm not quite ready to face the apartment on my own."

There was a little pause. "Fine," he said eventually. "I understand." He yawned. "I don't know about you, but I'm dead tired. I used muscles today that my body had forgotten it had. I'll see you in the morning, Kate."

She didn't know why she was so sure he was lying. Perhaps it was the languid grace of his movements that hinted at a body in absolutely perfect condition, except for the slight, lingering limp. Whatever his reason, she accepted the fact that he didn't want to spend any more time with her that evening. There was one question, however, that she had to ask him.

"Why did you say we were going to be married?" she asked.

A faint smile hovered at the corner of his mouth. "It seemed a rather effective way of taking the wind out of your father's sails."

"I'm sorry about what my parents said . . . about how they insulted you."

"Forget it. They know nothing about who I really am, so I don't feel insulted. It's you who should feel angry. Does your father often try to bully you? You don't want to marry that man he was talking about, do you?"

"Earle Darrin? No. I don't want to marry anybody." Her voice rang with fervent conviction.

"An unusual woman." Blake gave her another friendly smile. "Goodnight, Kate. Sleep well."

She had no reason to prolong the conversation. She wasn't even sure why she wanted him to stay. "Thank you for letting me spend the night here."

"You're welcome." He shut the door quietly behind him, and Kate wandered over to look out the window into the darkness of the overgrown yard. It was a long time before she turned away from the black, star-spangled night and climbed the stairs to bed.

· 4 ·

KATE COULDN'T REMEMBER another time in her life when she had enjoyed herself so much. She had been at the farmhouse for more than a week now, and Blake had long since stopped asking her if she wanted to go back to the city.

She spent her time cleaning the house, working methodically from the attic down to the dank and neglected basement. The work was hard, leaving her dirty, sticky, and tired at the end of each day. But she didn't mind. In fact, she loved every minute of it because she could see light and order and comfort springing up wherever she worked. Yesterday, Blake had produced a can of pale yellow latex paint, and she had painted the kitchen, transforming its old, gloomy walls into bright, cheerful ones. She could hardly wait to eat breakfast this morning. It would be like sitting inside a bowl of early spring sunshine.

Kate hummed to herself as she dressed in cutoff jeans and a simple green shirt that matched the color of her eyes. Blake had shown her his mother's old wardrobe, and she had found plenty of worn jeans and cotton tops that were perfect for the life she was leading.

She continued to sing as she made her bed. She had never been able to sing in tune, but she didn't care. Even if Blake heard her, he wouldn't laugh. He would just smile his usual lazy, tolerant smile and she would smile back, not at all embarrassed that she had sounded so terrible.

The kitchen was empty when she went downstairs, but she didn't care about that either. She never felt lonely in this house, although she had often felt oppressively alone in her parent's elegant Forsberg home and then the Milwaukee apartment she'd shared with Steven. Steven's family had lived on the floor above them in Milwaukee, and a housekeeper had come in every day to clean the already immaculate rooms. But Kate had always felt as though her life were lived behind an invisible wall of wealth that cut her off from normal human friendships. Her in-laws and the maid seemed like keepers of her prison, guarding her privilege and guaranteeing her loneliness.

Up here, even though the farm was so isolated, she never felt alone. Blake always seemed close at hand, filling her days with noise and laughter. Sometimes he worked on a repair project around the house. Usually he worked outside, painting the barns or changing the overgrown yard into a garden again. He worked so hard and so long that she wondered why the farm had ever been allowed to run down. He didn't give the impression of a man who enjoyed idleness. Occasionally she wondered if he had been unhappy, and if it was her presence which had spurred him into such hard work. On the whole, she tried not to think about her relationship with Blake. They were friends, she told herself, and that was enough.

She plugged in the percolator, admiring her painting efforts of the previous day as the smell of fresh coffee began to fill the room. It was wonderful to see the old house springing back to life. Already the property had regained the look of a place that was loved and cared for.

She stuck her head out the back door. Sure enough, Blake was already at work, putting a new pane of glass into a window of one of the small barns.

"Breakfast!" she yelled. She was twenty-five and she could never remember raising her voice before she met Blake. Nowadays, she always seemed to be shouting, her voice full of excitement and vitality.

Blake probably couldn't hear her, but he guessed what she was saying and waved his arm to indicate that he'd be coming up. She watched him walk across the yard, scarcely aware of how familiar his every movement had become to her. With a brief sense of shock, she realized that his limp was entirely gone. His injury, whatever it had been, was obviously a temporary one and probably fairly recent. She wondered what had caused the limp. Whatever it was, she knew she couldn't ask him. By tacit mutual consent, they kept their past lives utterly private.

She watched as Blake stopped by one of the hoses and turned it on, letting the cold water cascade over his neck and shoulders. All trace of pallor was entirely gone from his skin. He was so darkly tanned that it was almost impossible to imagine that ten days ago there had been traces of gray under his high cheekbones.

He grabbed his shirt from a nail by the back door and shrugged his wet shoulders into it. "Hi! That coffee sure smells good."

He relaxed into one of the kitchen chairs and looked appreciatively around the bright kitchen. "You did a great paint job, Katy. I scarcely recognize the gloomy old place."

She blushed. Nobody else had ever called her Katy. "Think nothing of it," she said lightly.

"It must be ninety degrees out there already. I guess we're heading for another thunderstorm before long."

"I'll use that as an excuse for not doing the laundry until

tomorrow. The tumble dryer doesn't work, you know." Kate smiled as she offered Blake a cup of the freshly-brewed coffee.

He drank deeply. "Let's not work today," he said. "I know a lake near here where the fishing's great. Let's pack a picnic lunch and drive there."

She had no idea how to fish, but the idea of a trip to a lake seemed fun.

"Is this a bonus for a week's hard labor?" she asked.

"Something like that," he agreed, his voice as light as her own.

They drove in Blake's old pickup, rattling over deserted roads that seemed to Kate to be more potholes than blacktop. She wouldn't admit to herself that she had imagined a romantic drive through the summer countryside, so she clenched her jaw shut, determined not to complain. After they had been driving in silence for a considerable time, she realized that Blake was laughing quietly to himself.

"What's the matter?" she snapped.

"Are your teeth rattling, Katy?"

"I wouldn't know," she replied tersely. "The rest of me is shaking so much that I can't feel my teeth any more."

She still heard the laughter in his voice, even though she wouldn't look at him. "It'll be worth it when we get there, you'll see," he said soothingly.

She turned to face him, planning to make some sharp retort, but the words died in her throat. His dark brown eyes glowed with teasing warmth and the harsh lines of his face were smoothed away in a smile of devastating charm. Her breath caught in a tiny gasp, and she quickly jerked her head away to stare out of the window. She had only just got used to thinking of Blake as her friend. She wasn't ready to commit herself any further. She couldn't think of anything to say until the silence was once again interrupted by Blake.

"This is it," he said. "The end of the road. We have to walk the last hundred yards." He parked the truck on a dirt patch, where the gravel road came to a dead end, and handed

Kate a woollen blanket. He reached into the back of the pickup and shouldered their fishing gear in one swift, easy movement. "I'll come back for the food," he said.

A narrow, deeply rutted path led down a rocky hill to the bank of the lake. The ground was dry underfoot, even up close to the water, and Kate had little difficulty scrambling down the shale-scarred slope, although the unaccustomed exercise left her panting. Blake, she noticed with irrational resentment, wasn't breathing any faster than usual. He hadn't so much as shifted the heavy bundle of fishing gear from one arm to the other.

"You're out of condition, old lady," he teased, when they finally stopped at the water's edge. "Haven't they heard about jogging in Milwaukee?"

"Yes. But we urbanites jog on smooth pavements, not on wilderness trails."

He laughed at her again. "One of these days, Katy, I'll take you into the real wilderness. This is just a beginner's playground." He took the blanket from her and spread it over a patch of rock-free grass. "Sit down and admire the view while I bring the food," he said. He touched her cheek casually with the tip of his finger. "I've noticed you always get grouchy when you're hungry."

He strolled away, moving effortlessly up the rocky escarpment, leaving Kate speechless. It was too long, she thought ruefully, since anybody had attempted to tease her. She'd forgotten how to laugh at herself. She'd played the role of earnest young society matron for so long that she'd started to believe in her own performance.

She lay down on the blanket, stretched out on her stomach, her head propped up on her hands. As Blake had promised her, the lake was a magnificent sight, well worth every bumpy mile of their journey.

"It's beautiful," she said when Blake returned with the box of food. He nodded his agreement and sat beside her in friendly silence. Together they looked at the opaline water, sparkling with white crests where the breeze whipped the surface into tiny waves. It was just possible to see the opposite shore, but Kate couldn't see it clearly enough to know if there were other fishermen or swimmers clustered near the beach. A solitary yachtsman tacked across a distant inlet. Otherwise, she and Blake seemed to be utterly alone.

"Was it worth a few rattled teeth?" Blake asked softly.

"Mmm . . . You know it was. . . ." She rolled onto her back, pulling up a stalk of grass and chewing contentedly on its moist, white root. "It's so peaceful here. Why hasn't anybody else discovered this place?"

"It's a private lake, accessible only to people who own property around the shore. The Property Owners' Association banned all motor boats years ago, which cuts noise pollution almost to zero and keeps the lake water clear for swimming."

"Are we trespassing?" Kate asked anxiously. She felt too relaxed to relish the thought of facing an angry property owner.

There was a slight pause. "No. As a matter of fact, I . . . that is my parents owned a piece of land here, and now it's mine. They were going to build a retirement home, but when my father died my mother lost all interest in moving."

"How sad. It's such a lovely spot."

"Yes." Abruptly, Blake changed the subject. "Let's eat lunch," he said. "What did you bring?"

"Chilled cranberry juice. Beer. Ham and cheese and some rolls I found in the freezer. Frozen fresh fruit salad that should be defrosted by now. For a housewife who hasn't been to the store for over a week, I think that's a pretty good selection."

"It's fabulous. You can sign on as my permanent household help any time you want."

Kate swallowed a tiny leap of anticipation. "Does the job have any special attractions? Domestic service isn't a fashionable occupation these days, you know."

"How about my wholehearted admiration? Is that special enough?"

She managed to laugh with convincing unconcern. "Not quite. Throw in a diamond a week and I'll consider applying for the position. I've grown attached to Windhaven Farm." She busied herself setting out paper plates and plastic cups. "What have you done with all the mosquitoes? It hardly seems like a picnic without them."

"I issued a royal edict commanding them all to buzz on the other side of the water," he replied lazily. "Does that fit your preconceived image of my autocratic personality?"

"Just about. But for once I'm glad the insects took your instructions to heart."

They ate their meal with hungry appreciation. When they had finished, Blake leaned back against a convenient boulder and stared up at the single cloud scudding across the sky. "This is the life," he said. "No sign of that thunderstorm. Let's forget about fishing. We could just lie on the blanket and stare at the water."

"The ground's too hard," Kate said quickly, not quite sure why she felt so uneasy at his suggestion.

"My shoulder makes a fantastic pillow."

"Which girl friend told you that?"

"Do you care?" he asked softly. When she refused to reply, he tugged gently on her arm. "Want to test it for yourself?"

"No, thank you." She jumped up with false energy. "I've been looking forward to catching a big fish. A trout or a bass."

Blake sighed. "I'm afraid there aren't any trout in this lake, and you're not likely to find bass either." He saw her crestfallen face and relented. "All right. You clear up the lunch, and I'll sort out the fishing gear."

Kate was already stacking paper plates back into the cardboard carton. She forced herself to ignore the strange, shivering excitement that had stirred in her body at the thought of lying in Blake's arms. She was crazy, she told herself as she watched Blake organize their equipment at the water's edge. Was she looking for an invitation to heartache? She rammed the plastic cups into a brown paper bag and walked down to the lake to rinse her hands in the clear water. Even this close to the bank, the water was surprisingly free of algae.

She straightened when she felt Blake's breath, warm against the nape of her neck. "Do you know how to fish?" he asked. His arm rested lightly against her body as he handed her the fishing pole, and she felt herself tighten with tension.

"Yes," she lied. "I know how to fish."

Blake took her answer at face value and moved away to cast his line deep into the lake. He sat, still and quiet, not bothering to look in Kate's direction.

Kate tried to remember the few pieces of information she had ever had on the art of fishing. She had spent one summer at a camp in Canada and remembered the rudiments. She knew just about enough to realize they were bait-fishing and that they were using open spinning-reel tackle. She loathed the sight of the worm wriggling on the end of her hook and cast her line deep into the water as quickly as she could. She had to repress a violent shudder as she heard the faint plop of the bait hitting the water. She scarcely had time to tighten her grip on the pole before she felt a pull on the hook, drawing her line taut.

"Blake!" she hissed, hardly able to believe her own success. "Help! I've caught a fish! What do I do now?"

"Reel it in," he said tersely.

"I can't. Not by myself."

He quickly secured his own fishing pole, then came to stand behind her, helping her reel in the struggling fish. She couldn't repress another gasp of distaste as Blake caught the desperately flapping fish firmly in his hands and proceeded to pull the hook out of its mouth, holding the fish firmly behind the head so that its movements were paralyzed. The fish dropped at her feet, thrashing wildly in the sun. Its skin was an ugly mottled gray, with bony spines radiating out along its dorsal fin.

"D-do I have to kill it?" Kate asked. "It isn't a bass, is it?"

"No, it's a sunfish. I suggest you throw it back. They're not very good to eat and I don't think you'd enjoy slitting its throat for no reason."

"No. I'll throw it back," she said quickly. She bent down and grasped the big fish, forcing down her loathing of the wet, slippery body. She hated to watch its frantic flopping as it gasped for oxygen. She tossed it back into the water, relieved when she saw it swim away into the deeper waters near the center of the lake.

"Do you think it will survive?" she asked.

"Probably." Blake sounded amused, although he looked at her with a hint of some other emotion. "Are you sure you still want to fish?" he asked. "You've turned a pale shade of green, and I have the distinct impression you're rooting for the fish."

"I am." She laughed to cover her embarrassment. "As a matter of fact, I wasn't telling the truth before. I don't know much about fishing, and actually I hate to eat fish."

Blake's silence was more eloquent than words. With exaggerated patience he showed her the best way of packing up her fishing gear. "I think I'll take a nap," he said when everything was finally stowed away. He moved the blanket slightly so that part of it was protected from the sun by the shade of an overhanging oak tree. He lay down, his head in the shadow, his darkly-tanned legs extended into the sun. Resting his head on one arm, he stretched out the other in casual invitation, and closed his eyes.

"You're welcome to the loan of my arm if you want a cushion," he said without opening his eyes. As far as Kate could tell, he was asleep before she even reached the edge of the blanket.

She hesitated only for a moment before dropping down to rest beside him. She looked at him covertly, thinking that his lean, muscled body appeared supremely arresting— graceful almost—even in sleep. She had to resist the impulse to reach out and run her hand through his hair. A thick, black strand had fallen forward over his forehead, giving an unexpected touch of vulnerability to his harsh features.

She became aware of her heart pounding deep inside her body, beating with an insistent rhythm that left her breathless. She lay down, resting her head on Blake's arm, and the smell of his hot skin filled her nostrils. She recognized the tight curl of need that pulled at her stomach. She was a woman, not a young girl, and she could identify physical desire even though Steven had taught her to think of herself as immune to sexual passion. Steven had never missed any opportunity to point out how unsatisfactory their lovemaking was, and she had accepted that the fault was all hers. Steven, after all, had a wide experience on which to base his unfavorable judgment.

She pushed the thought of Steven to one side, scarcely noticing that for the first time since her marriage she was able to dismiss him with no lingering feeling of guilt. They had married too young, and had been totally incompatible. The only redeeming feature of their marriage was that they had both been wise enough to agree not to have children. That decision, Kate thought wryly, was about the only responsible one they had ever made together.

She felt Blake stir against her side, and she turned so that her head rested on his chest. She could feel the rough prickle of his hair beneath the thin cotton shirt he wore, and she could no longer resist the urge to touch him. Her hand slipped inside his shirt, and she felt his heart beating strongly against her palm.

She sensed the abrupt movement of his head and realized that he wasn't asleep, but she couldn't move quickly enough to escape. He caught hold of her hand, trapping it beneath his own. His eyes locked with hers, and she knew it was useless to try to conceal her emotions. Her desire was written in the turmoil of her green eyes.

"Hello," Blake said huskily. "Did I remember to tell you this morning that you're beautiful?"

"Not that I recall," she murmured, her voice as husky as his.

There seemed no need to say anything more. Their bodies were saying it all. Slowly, she moved away from him, knowing that he would follow. She lay back on the blanket, no longer aware of the rough ground beneath her shoulders or the sunlight filtering through the branches of the oak tree. Her whole existence was concentrated on Blake: his dark eyes, his hands, his mouth. Even so, she was unprepared for the powerful shock of pleasure that filled her when he took her in his arms. His mouth touched hers, and she closed her eyes, feeling herself tremble in response to the pressure of his body.

His kiss was far too short to satisfy the new clamor of her senses. He lifted his head to look at her again, then his hand drifted slowly along her cheek, stroking the outline of her mouth with one sensitive finger. In a purely instinctive reaction, her body arched tightly against his, and her hands reached out to clasp around his neck.

For a moment she was frightened by the intensity of her own feelings. Blake had scarcely begun to make love to her, but already her body was quivering with needs and desires she had never experienced while married to Steven.

"Blake..." she murmured, although she didn't know herself why she needed to say his name.

"Yes, Kate?" His voice was tender and his fingers moved over her throat, caressing her skin until she no longer remembered what she had said or why she had spoken.

At last he bent his head again to kiss her, and her mouth answered his with a restless, yearning hunger. His tongue forced her lips apart and she welcomed the sensual intimacy of his possession. His body was hard with need, and her body burned with an answering fire.

She could hear Blake breathing with a rough, irregular sound, and it pleased her to know that she had the power to force him out of his usual iron control. His hand stroked her back with an urgency that heightened her arousal, and when he started to undress her, she thought of nothing except that she ached to feel his body pressed close to her naked skin. She murmured with soft pleasure when his tongue started to caress her breasts.

It was Blake who halted their lovemaking, pulling away from her with an abruptness that left her dazed and shaken. He sat up, tugging the sides of her blouse together, and it was a few seconds before she realized he was talking—not to her, but to a middle-aged man who had halted only a few feet away from them.

"What is it?" Blake asked curtly.

"This is private property. No picnics allowed here. Can't you read the signs? They're printed big enough." The older man's voice faded into a shocked silence as Blake stood up. "Mr. Har—"

"I'm Blake Koehler," Blake interrupted quickly. "I don't think we've ever met?"

"Er . . . no. We haven't met Mr. . . . er . . . Koehler. My name's Frank Brun. I'm real sorry I didn't recognize you. I didn't mean to interrupt anything."

Blake's reply sounded strangely wary to Kate's disoriented senses. "There's no reason at all why you should have recognized me; I'm hardly ever up here. My friend and I were just leaving, as a matter of fact."

The man made no comment on this obvious untruth. His only concern seemed to be to explain why he had intruded. "The thing is, Mr. Koehler, there's been trouble with groups of young people driving out from the city. They start barbecues and don't put out the fires, and we had one lot who dumped a huge can of oil into the middle of the lake. Don't have any idea why they did it, but it killed off a heap of real good fish. The Property Owners' Association told me and Sam to patrol the shore line. I saw a pickup truck parked on your land, and of course I didn't know you were in Wisconsin. We heard you were working in—"

"You were quite right to come and investigate," Blake interrupted again. "I didn't realize the lake had been discovered by tourists. I guess nobody would mind the occasional trespasser if only they would take care of the environment." He pulled Kate to her feet as he spoke, casually brushing a few stray wisps of grass from her cutoff jeans. "It's time for us to get back to my parents' farm."

"I'll help you to pack up," said Frank. "My son will be thrilled when I tell him I spoke to you today—"

"I'm going to escort Kate back to my pickup," Blake said, once again cutting across the man's words. Kate wondered if she was imagining the inexplicable tension that tautened Blake's body. "Perhaps you'd be kind enough to stack all the fishing gear into one pile?"

He didn't wait for the man to reply, and Kate noted his air of authority. He *expected* Frank to follow his instructions in a way that indicated he was accustomed to having his orders obeyed. She was too confused to give her muddled observations concrete shape. She just watched Blake and realized that ever since she had first met him, she had never seen him in any situation he didn't control. He put his arm around her shoulders, and it felt entirely natural to relax against him. "Ready?" he asked.

She nodded, waiting until they were out of earshot before asking, "Why did you want to get away from that man? What were you afraid he might say?"

Blake's look of astonishment seemed perfectly genuine. "You have a too-vivid imagination, Kate my sweet. I just thought you would prefer to get back to the privacy of the truck. It seemed to me you were having difficulty doing up the buttons on your shirt, and our friend Frank seemed to have a wandering eye." The teasing smile he gave her was tender enough to remove all sting from his words. They arrived at the gravel patch where he had left the truck, and he caught her face between his hands, turning up her chin so he could drop a brief kiss on the tip of her nose. "You're sunburned," he said. "Your nose is turning bright red."

"Oh no!" She craned her neck and peered ruefully in the wing mirror of the old truck. "I guess that's the penalty I have to pay for being so fair."

He ran his hand swiftly through her hair, which had long since lost all its bobby pins and cascaded in a rippling mass over her shoulders. "You're beautiful anyway, even with pink skin." He hesitated just for a moment, then brushed another brief kiss across her parted lips. He smiled wryly when her body arched involuntarily against his.

"If you want to know the truth," he said, "I had to make a polite excuse to get away from that over-eager investigator. Otherwise I would probably have punched him on the jaw. I didn't exactly appreciate the interruption."

"Neither did I," she whispered, and then blushed fiercely, appalled at what she'd said. She wasn't very skillful at casual flirtation, but she could guess that Blake was an expert. Kate was afraid she might find herself plunging into a relationship that was completely outside the range of her past experiences. She knew, instinctively but certainly, that if she let herself be drawn into an affair with Blake Koehler, she ran the risk of being badly hurt. Already, after such a short time, she found it impossible to imagine life without him at her side.

His gaze rested briefly on her troubled face. His own expression was once again impenetrable. She felt the fleeting touch of his warm lips before he opened the truck door. "Get in," he said firmly. "I'll collect our belongings from Frank."

She obeyed him because her feelings were in such turmoil that she found it difficult to reach any independent decision. During the past few days at Windhaven Farm she had learned to trust Blake as her friend. Now, the whole basis of their relationship seemed changed. Whatever she felt toward him, friendship was an inadequate word to describe the tumultuous state of her emotions.

She heard the sound of footsteps signaling his return, and her gaze followed him as he strode back up the slope, with Frank clambering along behind him. The two men loaded the gear into the rear of the truck, and once again she had the impression that Blake was determined to cut off any further conversation with the man.

Her suspicions seemed groundless as soon as Blake swung himself into the driver's seat. When he was near her, she found it difficult to think, and impossible to think rationally. Frank gave them a friendly farewell nod and walked away, presumably to continue his patrol. Blake turned on the ignition and put the pickup into gear without giving Frank another glance. He turned to Kate and ruffled her untidy hair.

"Tired?" he asked.

She shook her head. "How could I be? We didn't do anything."

"Unfortunately." He watched the color run up into her cheeks, then brushed his fingers across her face in a swift, tender caress. "I'm more than willing to pick up where we left off," he said. "At home nobody can interrupt us."

"Home," she repeated softly. "It's becoming too easy for me to think of Windhaven as home." She turned worried eyes toward Blake. "Sometimes I think we've been living in a fool's paradise for the past ten days. We've acted as though the rest of the world was nothing more than a troublesome dream, far over the horizon. I've enjoyed our dream and I don't want to wake up, but maybe it's time I went back to my apartment. I have to face up to reality. I have responsibilities waiting for me in the city."

His face was tense with some hidden emotion. "Your apartment isn't the only reality. You could stay with me." He hesitated, choosing his words carefully before he spoke again. "I'd like you to stay with me permanently, Kate. You've become very important to me."

A crash of thunder marked the end of his words, giving her a welcome excuse to avoid a reply. She had, in fact, no idea what she wanted to say. The first raindrops spattered on the windshield, and within seconds the truck was enveloped in a sheet of rain. Rivulets of cold water trickled into the truck before Kate could roll up the side window. The gravel road was rapidly turning to mud.

"Hell and damnation!" Blake exclaimed, peering through the window. "I didn't expect the storm to come from the east. I thought we could avoid it. I'll have to concentrate on the road or we'll miss the turnoff for the farm."

Kate was more than happy to remain silent, since it gave her a chance to think about what Blake had said. What did he mean when he said he would like her to stay with him permanently?

Lightning flashed, causing Blake's features to stand out in a harsh, unnatural glow. Kate shivered. All at once Blake seemed a total stranger. She was frightened by the knowledge that her feelings were already so involved with a man whose past remained a mystery.

The violence of the storm increased during the ride back to the farm. A perfect accompaniment, Kate thought grimly, for the emotional battle raging in her heart.

- 5 -

THEY WERE SOAKED to the skin by the time they reached
the shelter of the farmhouse, even though Blake parked the
pickup right outside the front door. The rain water ran off
their clothes and settled in little pools on the stone-flagged
floor.

It was chilly in the shadowed hallway, and Blake put his
arms around Kate, urging her into the kitchen. He found
a couple of clean towels and began to dry her hair so vig-
orously that it stuck out around her face in wild, spiky
confusion. They both started laughing when she caught sight
of herself in a mirror, and she was happy for no reason
except that they were together.

Deliberately, Kate pushed her problems to the back of
her mind. Just for once, she was going to allow her feelings
to overrule her common sense. She had lived all her adult

life according to her parents' rules. Surely it wasn't too much to want one afternoon . . . one night . . . when she could listen to the promptings of her own emotions.

Blake caught her face between his hands and turned it up to drop a kiss on her parted lips. "Why are you looking so solemn? What great problems have you decided to worry about now?"

She shook her head, not sure how to reply, and he kissed her again, tenderly. "I've come to the conclusion that driving with you is a hazardous occupation. You seem to attract thunderstorms." He ran his hands over her hair, smoothing it. "You look like a drowned rat."

"So do you!" she protested.

He smiled teasingly. "I wasn't complaining. Do you know your blouse is transparent now that it's wet?"

"Oh, no!" She pulled one of the towels out of his grasp and clutched it tightly in front of her.

"I liked the view better before," Blake said. "It reminded me of the night you arrived at Windhaven. Have you any idea how sexy you looked with that silk dress plastered to your body?"

"I had the impression you weren't very pleased to see me the night I arrived here," she murmured. She was hardly aware of the meaning of the words they were exchanging. She could feel her body shivering with excitement wherever his hands touched her.

"I wasn't, was I? I must have been out of my mind to shut the door when you were standing on the other side of it. Well, at least I've returned to sanity now." He pulled her into his arms, all trace of laughter vanishing from his eyes. "I want you so much, Kate. I want to love you. Don't make me wait any longer."

His hands continued to send ripples of pleasure everywhere they caressed. She could feel the hard wall of his chest through the loose-knit fabric of his shirt, and she wanted to be even closer to the warmth and strength of his body. Hesitantly, she swayed against him and, as she looked into his eyes, a strange, drowning excitement engulfed her.

Without another word, Blake bent his head, and she yielded herself to his kiss. He brushed her lips in the lightest, most fleeting of caresses, but it affected her like the touch of fire. She wondered how she had managed to survive for twenty-five years without ever before feeling fully alive.

He kissed her again, and this time there was no gentleness in his touch. His mouth moved passionately to possess hers, and the pressure of his kiss sent her head back against the support of his arm. His hands slid down her body, leaving a burning trail she could feel through the cool dampness of her clothes. Her hands moved up over his thighs and locked together in the small of his back, holding him closer. He pushed aside her shirt to kiss the hollow between her breasts, and she felt her whole body shudder in response. When he finally drew away from her, Kate gave a tiny, involuntary groan of protest.

"We should go upstairs," Blake said. "I want to make love to you in my bed. Although the way I feel right now, I don't think I'd notice where we were lying."

Once Blake stopped kissing her, all the old doubts had a chance to resurface. She stirred uneasily in his arms. "Blake, I'm not sure . . . I don't know if this is right . . ."

"I'm thirty-four years old, Kate, and you're twenty-five. Don't you think we're past the stage of playing games with each other's feelings?"

"Give me a little more time, Blake. There have been too many changes in my life recently. Sometimes I wonder if I know what I think about anything any more."

He continued to hold her gently, but firmly, within the circle of his arms. "I want to make love to you, Kate. I want to marry you. What else is there to say?"

"Marry me?" she repeated. "You want to marry me?"

A faint trace of color darkened the tan on his high cheekbones. "Yes," he said. "I never thought marriage would be important to me. I could never imagine committing myself to another person, but since I met you, Kate, everything seems to have changed. I want to see you wearing my ring. One day I know I'll want to see you pregnant with my child."

She was shaken by the conviction in his voice and by the strength of her own reaction to his words. She was flooded by a primitive wave of emotion at the thought of bearing Blake's child. But years of parental training prevented her from replying honestly, and she looked away from the intensity of his gaze, searching for some excuse not to commit herself.

"We don't know each other," she said at last. "We've been together less than two weeks. That's not long enough to fall in love."

"Isn't it?" He kissed her, softly at first, then with deliberately increasing passion. She knew her eyes were drowsy with desire when he finally lifted his mouth from hers.

"You see?" he said triumphantly. "Your body knows how you feel even if your mind refuses to face facts."

She walked away from his arms so that she was far away enough to think clearly. "People can't marry because they think they'll be good together in bed. We need to find things out about each other . . . talk about our pasts . . . meet each other's families, that sort of thing."

"I've met your parents," he said with a faint grin. "And I'm afraid mine are out of reach for formal introductions. You'll just have to take my word for it that they were thoroughly respectable citizens. Positive pillars of their community. Even their dairy cows loved them."

She laughed, with only a touch of frustration. "You know that wasn't what I meant."

He crossed over to her and took her hands, holding them tightly within his own. "Kate, we know the important things about one another. We enjoy each other's company; we always have things to talk about, and we seem to need to be silent at the same time. We listen to the same sort of music, and we've spent the last ten days laughing at the same jokes in old copies of magazines."

"But there's another world outside this farmhouse, and we both have to live in that world as well as with each other."

He put one arm around her waist, pulling her against his hard body. "Then at night we'll shut out the world and come back to each other. Don't try to deny it any longer, Kate. Why not admit that you want to make love to me as much as I want to make love to you?"

Why not confess the truth, Kate thought. Why couldn't she be honest and tell him how Steven had shattered her self-confidence. Why not admit that she was scared he would find her an inadequate lover. She shivered at the thought of Blake's rejection if she froze while he was making love to her. Even now, he had the power to wound her emotions more deeply than Steven had ever done. But she was tired of lies, she thought suddenly. Just for once, she wanted to be totally honest with another human being. She took her courage in both hands and drew in a deep breath, willing herself to carry through with her decision to admit the truth.

Kate's confession died in her throat as the kitchen door was flung open. If there had been a knock at the front door, neither of them had heard it. A pretty, vivacious teen-ager tumbled into the kitchen and ran across the floor, her hips wriggling provocatively in her skin-tight purple corduroy jeans. She flung her arms around Blake's neck and kissed him with evident expertise. Her pale lilac silk shirt came apart, revealing all too plainly that she wore nothing beneath it.

She continued to kiss Blake lingeringly, totally ignoring Kate. "Darling Blake," she said at last. "How could you run off and leave me? Don't you realize I've been *dying,* simply *dying* without you? And as for my father . . . Well, he's been total hell, darling. Absolutely and definitely total hell. . . ."

"Hello, Joni," Blake interrupted calmly. Kate was relieved to see that he disengaged the girl's hands from his neck and walked away from her to stand by the kitchen table. "I suppose the first question to ask is how you managed to find me."

"Darling, *I* remembered your name was Koehler even if my father didn't. You know what Sacha's like; he was in a towering rage one moment and in the depths of creative torment the next. So I saw if anything practical was going to be done, I'd have to do it. I came back to the States and ran a check on every Koehler who owns property in Wisconsin. Have you any *idea* how many Koehlers there are in this state?"

"It's a good, solid sort of name." Blake sounded faintly amused. "I'm still surprised you found me. How did you manage to remember my parents came from Wisconsin?"

"Darling, I remember *everything* about you. I knew you'd stay a thousand miles away from Los Angeles, and so all I needed was a little perseverance. You're forgetting we know one another rather... intimately."

"Yes, I know you very well, Joni. In fact, I think we'd better have a long, private talk before you say much more."

"Oh, Blake," the girl breathed, entwining herself around his body once again. "I've missed you so much."

Kate was shattered by the searing pain of jealousy that knifed through her. "I'm soaking wet," she said tersely. "I'm sure you'll both excuse me if I go and change."

"Don't leave for a minute." Blake put out his hand and pulled her close to his side. "This is Kate Danbury," he said, his voice softening fractionally as he spoke her name. "Kate, this is Joni Stein, Sacha's daughter."

"Hello, Kate." For the first time, the full power of Joni's baby-blue eyes turned directly on Kate. Her brown curls framed a young face that mingled smouldering sensuality and secret intelligence in about equal proportions. Kate was amazed to discover it was possible to dislike a person she had been introduced to only a moment ago. Before she could speak, Joni's cute little face wrinkled into an appealing grin. "How dreadful of me not to have seen you! How could I have missed noticing somebody so tall? But I was just so thrilled to find Blake!"

"Yes, I realize that," Kate replied dryly. "Hello, Joni." She forced herself to smile at the girl, and clenched her hands at her sides so she wouldn't pat self-consciously at her tangled mane of hair. Joni's pert prettiness left Kate feeling like a shaggy and overgrown beanpole. "I guess the rain must have stopped," she said, cursing herself for inanity as she uttered the words. "Blake and I got absolutely soaked when we came in, but you're quite dry."

"The rain ended half an hour ago. Heaven's, what have you two been doing for the past thirty minutes?"

"Kate and I were talking. I guess we didn't pay much attention to the weather."

"Darling, how utterly intense you must have been. Is Kate an old friend? Were you at school together?"

Blake's smile was indulgent. "Kate's ten years younger than I am, Joni. As I've no doubt you can see if you look closely."

Joni's not-so-baby eyes flashed in the direction of Kate's wedding ring. "You're married, Mrs. Danbury?"

"I'm a widow. But do, please, call me Kate."

Joni's hand crept inside Blake's shirt, where it started to stroke him seductively. "Dearest," she murmured in a perfectly audible whisper, "does Kate know all about you . . . about us? Or do I have to be discreet?"

Another white-hot shaft of jealousy pierced Kate's stomach, and although she saw Blake's angry gesture, she spoke without giving herself a moment to reflect. "I think you've misunderstood the situation, Joni. The appropriate question isn't whether I know about you and Blake. The question is, do you know about Blake and me? Do you know we're going to be married?"

"Married?" Joni turned pale and looked pleadingly at Blake. Kate avoided Blake's eyes, shocked into silence by the enormity of what she had just said. She could hardly believe she had allowed primitive sexual jealousy to goad her into saying something she would never have said in other circumstances. She flushed darkly, wondering how Blake would react to her hypocrisy. Two minutes before

Joni's arrival she had been protesting that they didn't know one another well enough to consider sleeping together, let alone getting married.

Blake's expression was unreadable as he examined Kate's heightened color, and she thought for a moment that he was going to deny her claim. "Yes," he said at last in response to Joni's question. "Kate and I are planning to be married. I'll tell you all about it in a minute, when we're alone." He looked at Kate with a smile she found impossible to interpret. "I think you should change out of those wet clothes before you catch a cold, Kate."

"What about dinner?"

"I'll pull a few packages out of the freezer to defrost."

"What about Joni? Shouldn't I prepare a room for her?"

"I'll entertain Joni. We have a great deal to say to one another, and I'm perfectly capable of showing her to the spare bedroom. I think you'd better take a hot shower right away."

"Yes," Joni interjected. "You look as though you could use a shower." Her smile was wide and innocent, and Kate bit back the angry retort that hovered on her lips. She'd allowed Joni to provoke her more than enough for one day.

"Excuse me," she said with all the dignity she could muster. "I'll see about dinner as soon as I've had a shower."

Kate clutched the old white towel more tightly around her body. For the first time since her arrival at Windhaven, she thought longingly of her wardrobe of expensive clothes, hopelessly out of reach in Milwaukee. She pushed her damp hair out of her eyes and examined the sparse rack of clothes, wishing that Mrs. Koehler's taste had run to something slightly more sophisticated than polyester pant suits. With a sigh, she selected a white turtleneck sweater and a faded denim skirt, knowing quite well that Joni would turn up at the dinner table in something fabulous.

As soon as she was dressed, Kate went downstairs to the kitchen. Baby lamb chops were already laid out to defrost

on the wooden table, together with a package of Chinese
pea pods and some frozen rice pilaf. Her thoughts chased
each other uselessly all the time she was preparing dinner.
Her emotions were in chaos, shaken out of the rigid control
she had exerted for the final two years of her lonely marriage. She felt frightened, but she wasn't quite sure what
she feared. Was she afraid Blake would take her rash words
seriously and assume they were getting married? Or was
she even more afraid that he would want nothing more to
do with her now that Joni had returned to his life?

She was strangely reluctant to admit the truth, even
though it kept forcing its way to the forefront of her mind.
She had vowed, after her disastrous relationship with Steven, that she would never become involved with another
man. But she guessed it was already too late to keep her
vow. She was hopelessly and irretrievably involved with
Blake Koehler, and the panic that clawed at her insides was
panic at the prospect of losing him.

She didn't hear him enter the kitchen. He dropped a
butterfly kiss on the nape of her neck, and an immediate
insidious warmth invaded her body.

"I didn't hear you," she said.

"You look beautiful," he replied, as if his words were
a logical response to her statement. "I wish you'd always
wear your hair loose like that. Until I met you, I didn't
know a woman's hair could be so erotic."

Kate turned to meet his dark gaze, but her hesitant words
of love were shattered by Joni's giggling. "Aren't you two
lovebirds planning to eat? I'm starving!"

Her voice was so friendly that Kate couldn't have explained why she was certain Joni's friendship didn't extend
a fraction of an inch beyond the surface. "You're in luck,"
she replied lightly. "Dinner's ready." She turned back to
give the lamb chops an unnecessary inspection, so that she
wouldn't have to look at Joni's fabulous purple jump suit.
The thin satin left the young woman's back entirely bare,
and her front was perilously protected by two narrow folds

of material. If she breathed too deeply, there would be nothing at all left to the imagination, Kate thought cynically, as she tugged angrily at her own dull white turtleneck.

"Do you need any help?" Blake asked softly.

"No, I'm fine." She scowled when he took her at her word and escorted Joni out of the kitchen, his hand resting with evident familiarity on her naked back.

The dining room was a gloomy little square that Blake and Kate had avoided as much as possible, preferring to eat their meals in the comfortable homeyness of the kitchen. Tonight, somebody had already lit two sets of candles, softening the bleak corners. Joni was seated in the center of the table and her vibrant features glowed in the mellow light. She was the inevitable focus of attention, but she complimented Kate on the meal and made some effort to include her in the conversation, as if repenting her earlier hostility.

"You know my father's Sacha Stein, the movie director," she remarked with a sweet smile. "And you probably know he's been nominated for an Oscar for his movie, *Time Zero*." She gave a little-girl sigh. "I'm so proud of my father."

As Joni spoke, Kate's memory was nudged by an elusive mental image. Why did that particular movie send chords jangling in her subconscious? Joni's voice intruded again before she could capture the fleeting memory. "You have *heard* about my father, haven't you? You have heard about Sacha Stein?"

"Yes, of course," Kate replied quickly. Seized by an imp of mischief, she glanced across the table, her eyes bright with secret laughter. "Sacha was the topic of my very first conversation with Blake. He simply wouldn't talk about anything else."

Blake's gaze locked with hers, his eyes dancing with shared amusement. Joni noticed the intimate exchange of glances and her expression hardened.

"I'm starring in my father's new movie," Joni said. "We're shooting the location shots in Fiji. Blake tells me you're just a housewife, Kate. Haven't you ever had a regular job?"

"I've never had a job that paid me a salary," Kate said quietly. She was interested in learning more about Joni's career, so she managed to swallow the several angry retorts that sprang to her lips. "Please tell me something about your own work," she said, glad that years of careful social training had left her adept at handling awkward guests, even when her own feelings were in turmoil.

"I'm playing a very demanding role as a teen-age criminal. My father believes that few women my age would be able to handle the part, and without Blake—"

"This will be Joni's first movie," Blake interrupted smoothly. A furious glance, which Kate didn't understand, flashed between Blake and Joni. Joni started to pick nervously at her food, while Blake resumed the conversation. "Joni's been acting on TV shows since she was a tot. I swear Sacha had her signed up to advertise baby lotion before she left the maternity ward."

"How interesting. Television always seems such a glamorous workplace to people like me on the other side of the camera. Is it good training for a movie career?"

"I act as naturally as I breathe," Joni replied, and for once Kate didn't doubt her sincerity. "I find it hard to talk about techniques because so much of what I do seems to be instinctive." She appeared to regret the honesty of her reply, for she flashed a spiteful look in Kate's direction and added with false sweetness, "I can't imagine what it must be like to sit at home all day with nothing to do except bake cookies and get fat. I've always thought women should have a career, don't you agree, Blake? How can women help becoming boring if all they do is poke around at home?"

Blake looked thoughtfully at Kate's heightened color. "A woman isn't necessarily empty-headed just because she doesn't work outside the home," he said. "Being a homemaker is always time-consuming, and I'm sure it can be very fulfilling for the right woman."

"Blake, you can't be serious!" Joni's nose wrinkled into an enchanting expression of disgust. "I can see what that monstrous man wants to do," she said, turning a pseudo-sympathetic gaze toward Kate. "He's decided to marry a woman who's already resigned to permanent domesticity. I'm warning you, Kate. Once you're married, he'll keep you under his thumb in the kitchen while he has fun out in the world. Are you *sure* you want to marry him on those terms?"

Kate's fragile control over her temper finally snapped. "That isn't precisely the way I see our marriage working out, Joni. I said I'd never held a paying job, but that doesn't mean I've spent my whole life as a decorative doormat. I have a college degree in special education, and I work four hours a day, five days a week at the Center for Autistic Children in Milwaukee. I wasn't paid because I didn't need the money, and I donated my salary back to the Center."

There was a tiny pause, but Joni recovered quickly. "How *incredibly* dedicated you must be, Kate. But of course you do look as if you're an earnest sort of person." Joni managed to make the compliment sound thoroughly insulting. She stretched delicately, leaning back in her chair so that the candlelight played over the creamy fullness of her breasts. The strips of purple halter provided less and less cover as she wriggled in the chair, yawning discreetly.

"Blake, darling, do you remember when my father gave that marvelous party in Bella's house?"

"Yes," said Blake.

The single word was all the encouragement Joni needed, and she launched into a lengthy stream of reminiscences, all of which she seemed to find uproariously funny and all of which were entirely meaningless to Kate.

Blake joined in Joni's laughter, but his eyes scarcely left Kate's face. She reveled in the knowledge that he was hardly bothering to disguise his desire to be alone with her. A tiny seed of hope planted itself in her heart. Maybe he really liked her. Her. The person she was. She turned the idea over in her mind wonderingly, letting Joni's words ebb and flow in a ripple of background noise.

The meal was suddenly at an end, the candles blown

out, and the dishes carried back to the kitchen. Kate had no idea what Blake had served for dessert. She had been aware of nothing but the physical tension growing between Blake and herself. She was startled when she heard her voice volunteer to make coffee. She hadn't realized she was still functioning normally.

"Thanks, but no coffee for me," Blake said. "It's been a long day and I'm about ready for bed. How about you two?"

"At this hour?" Joni squeaked. "Blake, it's only ten o'clock!"

He laughed. "Early bedtimes aren't a sin, you know. They're not even against the law."

Joni sighed and cuddled her half-naked body against his. "If I have to go to bed at this ungodly hour, aren't you going to come with me?" she asked and her wide, innocent eyes stared mistily into his.

"I'll escort you to your room," he replied. "Coming, Kate?"

"Yes."

They walked upstairs, Kate trailing behind, until Blake came to a halt outside the door of the third bedroom.

"Goodnight, Joni," he said. "Sleep well."

She looked at him with blatant appeal in her eyes. "Will you go back to Fiji, Blake? Please say you'll come back with me."

"I've already called Sacha and said I'll be going back." He held Joni's hands within his own and pulled her forward to kiss her quickly on her full, pouting lips. "Stop worrying, Joni, and get some rest."

She gave a short, bitter laugh as Blake crossed the narrow hallway to stand beside Kate. "Stop worrying?" she said. "We've all been worrying about the wrong things. Sacha had no idea what was bothering you, did he? The accident was just an excuse to leave Fiji . . . to get back to *her*."

"You promised me something when we spoke earlier," Blake said quietly. "Please don't forget."

"Promises! Who the hell cares about promises." Joni dashed her hand across her eyes, and Kate was astonished to see tears spiking the ends of the young woman's lashes.

"You were right to come and get me," Blake said, ignoring her outburst. "I'm grateful to you, Joni. You were right to remind me that I have obligations waiting for me in Fiji."

"What about her? What about Kate?" This time, Kate was sure Joni didn't mean her muffled question to be overheard.

"She can be with me in Fiji as easily as here. Kate will make no difference to anything, Joni, I promise you."

"Sure." Joni turned away with an angry toss of her curls. "For God's sake take her into your bedroom, Blake. I know it's what you've done every other night, so don't pretend for my sake." Without looking at Kate, she slammed the door of the guest room behind her.

Kate turned quickly, but not quickly enough. Before she could shut her bedroom door, Blake had stepped inside the room. He closed the door and walked briskly to the bed, flipping the switch on one of the bedside lamps.

She stood by the window, watching him in tense silence, and he glanced at her with a faint, sardonic smile. "You don't have to look so nervous, you know. I'm not planning to force you into my bed simply because Joni assumes we've been sleeping together. I just want a chance to talk to you privately."

Kate tried to look more nonchalant than she felt. She sat down on a hard wooden chair some distance from the bed. "I have to apologize," she said stiffly, keeping her gaze averted from Blake's lean body. "I don't know why I said we were getting married. It was a crazy thing to do."

"Was it? I hoped it might be the truth. I've spent the whole evening wondering how long I'd have to wait before I could get you alone to ask you if you meant what you said. I realized Joni had provoked you."

Kate finally looked at him, her green eyes shadowed

with confusion. "Why did Joni come here, Blake? Why are you so important to her?"

"She wants me back in Fiji, and she's a single-minded young woman. Despite all her efforts to suggest otherwise, Kate, we've never been lovers. If that's what you're worried about, you can forget it. Joni's an actress, and she needs an audience the way other people need food or friendship. Right now, she's decided to play the part of a betrayed lover, plotting her revenge. She's a good actress, but don't fall into the trap of thinking her performance conceals genuine feelings."

"Why is she so desperate for you to go back to Fiji?"

Blake was silent for a moment or two. "For professional reasons," he said at last. "The movie she's working on has a lot of action and quite a bit of violence. I was involved with some of the stunts before I left Fiji. . . . Underwater scenes, that sort of thing . . . Joni wants me to go back. I've done a lot of work with her father over the years, and she's used to seeing me around the set. She's as insecure as every other talented performer, and she has the idea that she acts better when I'm around."

"I can't quite see you in the role of nursemaid."

Some of the tension seemed to leave Blake's taut shoulders. His mouth twisted into a faint smile. "No," he admitted. "It isn't my favorite role."

Kate forgot all about keeping her distance from the dangerous intimacy of the double bed. She walked swiftly across the room, taking hold of Blake's hands in her eagerness to convey her point. "But you will go back to the movie, won't you? Whatever your quarrel was with Sacha, it isn't worth throwing away your career. I'm so glad my father was wrong and that you can find work as a stuntman. It must be a wonderfully exciting way to make a living."

"Yes, it is." He stood up, thrusting his hands through his hair. "I've already called Sacha to say I'll go back to Fiji," he said slowly. "Will you come with me, Kate?"

She drew in her breath, but he gave her no chance to

reply. "Oh, God, Kate," he said and his voice was thickened by desire. "I can't wait while you make up your mind. I want to make love to you now."

She shut her eyes, instinctively swaying against him, and she felt his breath mingle with her own. "Kiss me, Blake," she murmured. "I want you to kiss me."

"Oh, God!" His mouth covered hers with the force of an explosion. There was no lingering gentleness in the way he forced her lips apart, and he made no effort to conceal the intensity of his need. For a split second, her body froze in rejection, but as soon as Blake sensed her withdrawal, his kiss softened into a caress. Slowly, her body melted against his as he pulled her down beside him on the bed. He pushed aside the white cotton sweater with impatient fingers, and his lips trailed over her breasts while his hands stroked her body into surrender.

"I need to make love to you," he whispered. "I want to possess you *now*."

She knew she ought to stop him before he discovered for himself that she was useless as a lover. Her friendship with Blake was too important to be destroyed on the rock of an unsatisfactory sexual relationship. But her body trembled with a need she had never experienced before, and she parted her lips in an involuntary gesture of surrender.

He slipped the white sweater over her head and quickly unfastened the buttons of her skirt, pushing the faded denim over her hips and discarding it in an untidy heap at the foot of the bed. She waited for her body to freeze into its usual icy response, but Blake's mouth roamed over her naked skin and wherever he touched, passion grew.

A warm, insidious ache blossomed slowly inside her. She heard herself moan with soft pleasure as Blake's hands stroked her naked breasts, and beneath the tough skin of his palms, her nipples hardened with desire.

Scarcely able to believe her own eagerness, she reached for his shirt, pushing it aside so that she could rest her cheek against the prickle of dark hair curling on his chest. She

allowed her fingers to trail downward over the flatness of
his stomach as her eyes absorbed the strong lines of his
face. Even at this moment of passion there was a haunting
austerity in the tautness of his skin as it stretched over his
high cheekbones. The tips of her fingers traced the harsh
angles of his face, and detected a shadow of beard darkening
his cheeks. She pressed her open mouth against the rough
skin, teasing the faint stubble with her lips.

He made a low sound, deep in his throat, as he gathered
her closer to the hard strength of his body. His touch seared
her skin, and she whispered little words of desire against
his mouth.

"Love me, Blake," she murmured and the deliberate
restraint of his caress immediately became a fierce kiss. He
forced her mouth apart, probing deeply with his tongue.

"Kate, how beautiful you are," he murmured huskily.
"Your body is made for loving."

His words removed the final, fragile barrier of restraint
between them. He kissed her eyelids with burning lips, then
scorched a trail of kisses over her throat and across her
breasts. Kate was filled with a passion that ran through her
veins like liquid fire, heating her body with a dark flush of
need.

She knew that only Blake could fill the aching emptiness
deep inside her body, and when he possessed her at last,
she thought her whole being might shatter in the deep, velvet
darkness of fulfillment.

Afterwards, he held her close and smoothed the damp
tendrils of hair from her face. "Kate," he said softly when
they had been silent for a long time. "It's never been that
way for me before."

Happiness blossomed inside her. "Nor for me," she whispered and turned her face away because she was still shy
of expressing her emotions. "Blake . . . it was . . . with
Steven . . ."

"Hush," he said, with unexpected harshness. She looked

up at him, and his tight features relaxed again as he took her into his arms. "Hush, don't try to explain. We have all the time in the world for explanations."

She awoke in the middle of the night and stirred restlessly against his body, unused to feeling the warmth and hardness of a man's body next to her own. She stared at his profile, still arrogant even in sleep. She was teased by some persistent, elusive memory that nagged at the edges of her consciousness and would not leave her in peace. Suddenly, Blake was no longer asleep. His gaze locked with hers, and wordlessly he reached for her, drawing her roughly against his hard, sinewy body. She responded to his silent lovemaking with an almost desperate intensity, the nagging doubt temporarily forgotten.

He spoke only when their passion was spent, and she was once again lying still and safe in his arms. He brushed his mouth across her eyelids. "When will you marry me, Kate? For my sanity's sake, it has to be soon."

There was no more doubt in her mind, only a great and growing happiness. "Whenever you want," she said softly.

"I want it to be today," he said. "But I guess the state of Wisconsin will make us wait a little longer than that. I'll make arrangements for the end of this week. That's about as long as I can wait."

Lying in his arms, there seemed nothing strange in marrying a man she had known for less than a month. "Mrs. Koehler," she murmured and laughed under her breath. "I'm going to be Mrs. Koehler." And she fell asleep again, cradled contentedly against Blake's strong shoulder.

- 6 -

IT WAS RAINING when Kate awoke the next morning, not the torrential outburst of yesterday's thunderstorm, but the steady gray downpour of rain settling in for the day. She turned back from the gloomy view outside the bedroom window and found Blake's gaze resting on her.

"Hello," he said softly.

"Hi!" She felt her breath tighten with an upsurge of love, but she forced herself to smile casually. She mustn't let him know how important he was to her. She knew it wasn't safe to love anybody as much as she was starting to love Blake. Her relationship with her parents had taught her early in life that loving people left you open to hurt, and she didn't want Blake to hurt her. When she spoke, she was careful to keep her voice light.

"Summer seems to be over for a while," she said. "I hope you weren't planning to work outside. The yard looks as if it's turning itself into a temporary swimming pool."

Blake smiled lazily. "I hadn't planned on working anywhere, least of all the yard. I was hoping to spend the day in bed. The company in here last night was terrific." He raised one eyebrow in an unspoken question, then gave a mock sigh. "No? Well, I guess it was too much to hope you'd be as enthusiastic as I am." He stretched, then threw off the bedcovers, grinning when he saw the color flood into her cheeks for the second time. "I'm sorry my robe is in the other bedroom," he said. "But you do blush delightfully."

Before walking quickly across the linoleum-covered floor, he kissed her fleetingly and gave another exaggerated sigh. "Since you're already dressed, you'd better go downstairs while my intentions are still honorable. Otherwise we'll never get to Milwaukee today. We have to start making arrangements for our wedding."

Kate allowed herself another minute in his arms, then walked with determination toward the bedroom door. "I'll see you downstairs," she said, her voice not nearly as cool as she would have liked it to be. She slipped into the corridor before Blake could entice her back into bed. He would find her all too easy to persuade.

She had finished preparing the coffee when Blake came downstairs, followed by Joni, who was dressed this morning in white denim designer jeans and a baby-blue sweater that exactly matched her eyes. Kate scarcely managed to conceal her flash of envy. "Did you sleep well, Joni?" she asked with as much friendliness as she could muster.

"Yes, thank you."

Kate unplugged the percolator and carried it with her to the breakfast table. "I'm sorry we can't offer you fresh milk or eggs for breakfast. We . . . er . . . don't seem to have had a chance to go grocery shopping recently."

"I only drink black coffee in the mornings," Joni replied.

Kate tried to think of some polite response, but her mind was a blank. Fortunately Blake spoke before the uncomfortable silence could stretch out too long. "Kate and I are going back to Milwaukee today, Joni. If you don't want to stay at the farm alone, may I help you find a hotel in the city?"

"There's no reason for me to stay in a dead place like Milwaukee," Joni said curtly. Recovering her poise, she smiled sweetly at Blake. "Now that I've persuaded you to come back to Fiji, darling, there's nothing to keep me in the States. I've already decided that I'd better fly back to Sacha before he throws the fit to end all fits."

"Please tell him we'll be joining you at the beginning of next week," Blake said. "Tell him I'll be ready to start work right away."

"When and where are you having the wedding ceremony?" Joni asked.

"In a judge's chambers at the town hall, I guess." Blake gave a quick shrug of his shoulders. "We don't have time to arrange anything more elaborate."

Joni's expressive features revealed her scorn for such a simple ceremony. "Well, it's your lives, darling, but it's all a bit dreary, isn't it?" Without waiting for a reply, she yawned and smiled, revealing two rows of perfect white teeth. "I wish you both all the happiness you could possibly expect. I'll call Sacha tonight so he can send you a dozen orchids or do whatever it is people are supposed to do at weddings." She gave another graceful little wriggle. "I'm not exactly *into* weddings myself."

"Don't tell Sacha about my marriage plans," Blake said curtly. "I'll telephone him myself . . . after the ceremony. Kate and I want to have a very quiet wedding, and Sacha would turn it into a three-ring circus."

Kate wondered briefly why Sacha would have any special interest in Blake's wedding, but the question faded quickly from her mind. She could scarcely believe it was her wedding, her marriage to Blake Koehler, that was being discussed so casually across the breakfast table. Panic grew in her at the thought of how rashly she had committed herself. She felt Blake's eyes, forcing her to look up, and when she met the powerfulness of his dark gaze, she was suddenly calm again. Of course she was doing the right thing in marrying the man she loved. What did it matter if they hadn't known each other very long? In the final analysis, even Joni's jealous dislike was entirely irrelevant. All that mattered was how she felt about Blake and how he felt about her.

A great weight seemed to be lifted from Kate's shoulders. She was able to smile quite naturally at Joni. "If you've all finished breakfast," she said, "I guess we should get ready to leave. I have a pile of things to do once I'm back in Milwaukee."

Joni's eyes rested speculatively on Kate's face for an instant. Then she was on her feet, smiling at Blake with all her usual vivaciousness. "Can you help me bring down a couple of suitcases and stow them in my car? I can see it's time for me to leave you two alone." She allowed her mouth to droop with a hint of pathos. "I probably shouldn't have come. You didn't want me here."

Blake draped his arm around her sagging shoulders. "I've already told you how grateful I am that you came. You made me realize it was past time for me to get back to work."

"Really Blake? I really helped?" Joni's blue eyes sparkled with a misty sheen of tears.

"Really," he replied with only the faintest touch of irony. They left the room, his arm still around her shoulders. A few minutes later Kate heard the sound of tires squealing on the gravel driveway as Joni propelled her rented Corvette into action.

That afternoon Kate and Blake went to her apartment in Milwaukee.

"Do you like it?" Kate asked Blake as he prowled around

the elegant living room. "Do you... Are you planning to stay here with me until the wedding ceremony on Friday?"

Blake slowly turned back from his observation of Lake Michigan. "No, I can't stay," he replied at last. "I have to go back to Windhaven if I'm going to put the farm on the market."

Kate nodded. They had discussed selling the farm during the drive into the city. Blake fell silent for a minute, then walked swiftly across the room to take her hands, seeming uncharacteristically ill-at-ease. "Kate," he said, "there's something I ought to tell you. Something you should know before we get married."

She was immediately afraid. Hadn't she suspected all along that this wonderful, swiftly-flowering relationship was too good to be true? "What should I know?" she asked, her attempt at casualness a miserable failure. "Have you forgotten to mention a couple of wives tucked away in Los Angeles?"

"Nothing like that. I told you yesterday that, until I met you, I never considered marrying anyone. Kate, what I have to tell you is about my work... my profession...."

The phone shrilled into the tension of the room, making them both jump. "Hell!" he exclaimed, under his breath, turning away.

She wished she could just ignore the persistent ringing, but Blake obviously had no intention of speaking until she had answered the phone. She hurried into the study, not sure whether the interruption was a welcome reprieve or not.

"It was Betty Bergdorf, the trustee for Steven's estate," she said when she returned to the living room a few minutes later. Blake was still staring fixedly out of the window, and she wondered what he would say when he finally turned around to face her. "She's been trying to reach me for days," Kate continued. "She wants to see me this afternoon, and I said I would go to her office if you don't have any other plans."

He turned around at last. "No," he said. "I have to get back to Windhaven. You ought to see Ms. Bergdorf, especially since you'll be leaving the country as soon as we're married."

"What was it you wanted to tell me, Blake? You said there was something I ought to know about you before we get married."

His hesitation was so slight as to be almost imperceptible. "I wanted to talk to you about our finances," he said and his voice sounded so completely relaxed and natural that Kate could not justify her continuing uneasiness. "I let your parents give you the wrong impression the other day," Blake said. "I'm not bankrupt. I'm not even hovering on the poverty line. Stuntmen are well paid, you know. I don't want you to think you have to change your life-style or your financial plans because you're marrying me. I can support you and any children we may have. Make sure Ms. Bergdorf understands that."

Kate relaxed as he finished speaking, confident she had understood the faint lines of tension etched on his face. Blake Koehler, she guessed, was not a man to welcome the prospect of living on his wife's income.

"I'm delighted to hear I'm marrying a prosperous gentleman!" she teased, and this time she was more successful in keeping her voice light and unconcerned. "I'm glad I can reassure my parents that you aren't marrying me for my money."

He smiled faintly. "No," he agreed. "That's not why I'm marrying you." The passion in his dark gaze melted Kate's heart and made her legs feel shaky. She moved into his arms so naturally that it seemed as if they had known each other for years. Even when Blake drew back from their long, passionate kiss, he continued to hold her close.

"Will you trust me to deal fairly with the whole question of our finances?" he said. "We're so pushed for time that I don't want to get involved in estate planning right at this moment. Or do I need to come and see your Ms. Bergdorf to make sure she understands my financial intentions are strictly honorable?"

"Of course I trust you! I'd hate you to feel obliged to discuss your financial position with Betty. It's not necessary, and money is such a boring thing to talk about."

Blake's smile was suddenly hard. "I think that's the first time I've heard you sound like the very rich young woman you actually are. Money, Kate, is only a bore when you have so much of it that you need to pay other people to look after it for you."

She laughed, half-annoyed, half-embarrassed. "Now *you* sound like my father!"

The constraint left his face, and he kissed her quickly. "Your father can't always be wrong," he said, moving away from their embrace. "Kate, I have to get out of here, or I'll be taking you to bed, and we simply don't have time for an afternoon spent in the bedroom."

"Are you rejecting me before the honeymoon even begins?" she asked, able to tease him now that the moment of strain was over.

He drew in a sharp breath. "You know damn well I'm not. But I want to marry you lawfully on Friday, Kate, and that doesn't leave much time for making practical arrangements."

"When will I see you again?"

"Not until Thursday evening, I'm afraid. I'll take you out for a fabulous celebration dinner at Milwaukee's best restaurant, if you'll tell me which one that is."

"But Thursday is such a long way away! It's the night before our wedding!"

"Darling Kate, it's scarcely more than forty-eight hours from now! Somebody has to spend the next two days running around government offices, filling out forms and signing official declarations. Which reminds me. Can you give me your passport and your birth certificate? Somehow I have to persuade the authorities to give you an entry visa for the Fiji Islands. If I can manage *that* within forty-eight hours, you'll know for sure you're marrying Superman!"

She laughed. "I'll look out for your cape in our honeymoon luggage. But please don't pack your tights. I can't stand men in tights."

He glanced up, his gaze locking with hers. "I'll miss you," she whispered breathlessly, all laughter fading from her expression.

"And I'll miss you like hell." His kiss was hard, almost angry in its intensity. "Please find your passport. I have to get away from here while my willpower holds out."

"At least we managed to get our blood tests done on the way into the city," she said as she rummaged through bureau drawers. She finally managed to find her passport and a copy of her birth certificate. "What are you going to do about a car? Do you want to borrow mine?"

"No, I'll rent something. We'll need a car to drive to O'Hare after we're married. We can't have your Porsche standing in the airport parking lot for weeks on end." He was already striding to the main apartment door as he spoke. "Are you sure you can make all the arrangements so that you're ready to leave the country on Saturday?"

She nodded. "I'm used to traveling overseas."

"I'll pick you up on Thursday at seven."

"You may not recognize me," she said provocatively. "You've only seen me dressed in jeans. And you keep reminding me that the night I arrived at the farm I looked like a drowned rat."

"But you're the only sexy drowned rat I've ever encountered. Take care, Kate." He shut the door firmly, and the silence of the apartment echoed hollowly in her ears.

It was a relief to escape from the loneliness of her apartment into the organized frenzy of Betty Bergdorf's office. Ms. Bergdorf, a short, wild-haired young woman, looked nothing like the stereotyped image of a successful female financial wizard. Her looks, however, belied her efficiency. She greeted Kate warmly, and plunged into the details of their discussion with the bare minimum of courteous preliminaries.

"The legal arrangements for establishing the Foundation are almost complete. If you want to change your mind about handing such a considerable amount of money over to charity, Kate, now is the moment to do it."

"No, I don't want to change my mind," Kate replied. "Steven died much too young, and I don't want to profit financially from his death." She hesitated a moment before continuing. "Steven was so healthy that he hated to be around sick people," she said. "But he was very interested in my work with the children at the Center, and he made several donations to research into the cause of birth defects." Steven's genuine interest in her work with autistic children, Kate thought, was about the only interest they had shared by the time he died.

She realized Betty Bergdorf was looking at her speculatively, so she added quickly, "Steven always planned to make a major donation to the Center, so I'm only carrying out his wishes."

"I'm sure the Board of Directors at the Center will be delighted to learn that you haven't changed your mind. I've followed your instructions and made certain that the Principal at the Center knows nothing about your plans. But Kate, she'll have to be told soon. The Principal is always involved in budget discussions, and she can't be kept ignorant of the fact that you're planning to make a major contribution to the Center's income."

"I understand," Kate said. "When we first discussed this endowment, I was afraid it would be embarrassing for me to work with the other teachers and therapists if they knew Steven's money was paying part of their salaries. But my plans have changed recently. I'm going to resign from my job." She couldn't control the faint flush of happiness that ran into her cheeks at the mere thought of her forthcoming marriage.

Betty Bergdorf's deceptively innocent face expressed

sudden interest. "May I know why your plans have changed?"

Kate laughed a little self-consciously. "I'm getting married on Friday," she said. "And my husband and I will be flying out of the country the next day. We'll probably be gone for several weeks. And in any case, his permanent home is in Los Angeles."

"That's wonderful news!" Betty exclaimed with evident sincerity. "I won't say congratulations, because your future husband is the person to be congratulated. He's a lucky man. Is he somebody I know?"

"No, we only met recently. His name's Blake Koehler."

"I certainly wish you both every happiness. Perhaps he could have lunch with me some time when you get back from overseas?"

Kate laughed. "I'm not deceived by that ingenuous expression, Betty. I know you want to check him out and make sure his financial prospects are sound."

Betty Bergdorf looked as close to embarrassment as it was possible for her to do. "Even though you've handed Steven's fortune over to charity, you're still a wealthy young woman, Kate. I'm your financial adviser, so you have to expect me to look out for your interests."

Kate stood up and reached out to shake Betty's hand warmly. "Of course I understand, and Blake will no doubt be delighted to come in and be inspected. Good-bye, Betty. If we weren't having such a very small wedding, you'd be at the top of my guest list."

As she escorted Kate through the warren of office cubicles, Betty said casually, "Kate, this doesn't affect your personal financial standing in any way, because since your marriage all your funds have been invested in Steven's family companies. But the financial community here in Milwaukee is beginning to hear rumors that everything isn't quite all it should be with Forsberg Industries."

"You mean with my father's companies?" Kate couldn't conceal her astonishment.

"Yes." Betty's voice remained deceptively casual. "I heard, Kate, from a couple of impeccable sources, that your father's health isn't all that good either. And, of course, he's always been a man who finds it difficult to delegate, so there's no successor groomed and ready to take over."

Kate felt a surge of fear, then common sense displaced the brief moment of uncertainty. "Betty, I saw him ten days ago, and I can assure you he looked in his usual roaring health." She smiled ruefully at the memory. "In fact, *roaring* is just about the best way to describe him."

"I'm glad to hear you're confident that the rumors have no foundation in fact," Betty replied and changed the subject smoothly. "Don't forget, Kate. We have a lunch date as soon as you get back from your honeymoon."

Kate didn't bother to explain that her journey with Blake was a business trip rather than a prolonged honeymoon. She parted from Betty well satisfied with the progress made in establishing the trust. It was reassuring to think that one totally worthwhile project had been salvaged from the wreck of her marriage to Steven. His death had been tragically unnecessary, but at least her inheritance could give several children new hope for correct treatment and education.

It was late afternoon when she arrived back at the apartment, but she guessed that Mrs. Kearney, the Principal at the Center, would still be working. The special education facility at the Center closed down during July and August so that Kate and most of the other instructors could take a vacation. Other departments remained open, however, so that a few children at a crucial stage in their treatment could remain under trained supervision. Mrs. Kearney would almost certainly be working away in her poky little office. Kate realized with a pang of guilt that her own unexpected resignation, so close to the reopening of school, would leave a gap in the Center's resources. Autistic children needed constant supervision and one-on-one remedial teaching if they were to make any progress, so the presence of each and every teacher was vital. She tried to soothe her conscience with the hope that some of Steven's money would be released in time to provide extra funds to pay for a fully-trained replacement teacher. Nevertheless, it wasn't easy to pick up the phone and dial the Principal's private office number.

Mrs. Kearney, far from accusing Kate of deserting her charges, sounded so generously delighted at the prospect of her forthcoming marriage that Kate's guilt actually increased. Stumblingly, she tried to tell Mrs. Kearney of the funds the Center would be receiving, implying that the money was being distributed under the terms of Steven's will. She eventually put down the phone with Mrs. Kearney's rapturous thanks still ringing in her ears.

She had thought it would be impossible to sleep, but the events of the previous two days had left her more exhausted than she knew, and she slept dreamlessly until eight the next morning. She showered and dressed briskly, not allowing herself to think about the day ahead of her. She knew she had an obligation to drive up north to Forsberg and break the news of her forthcoming marriage to her parents. She was not, however, looking forward to the trip.

A phone call to her father's offices confirmed that her parents were both in town. She left word with her father's secretary that she would be arriving about lunchtime. Not for the first time, she thought how absurd it was that she felt constrained to make appointments with a secretary to see her own parents. When Blake and she had children, she vowed silently, she would never be too busy to take a telephone call.

She drove unseeingly along the familiar roads to the small town of Forsberg, her mind flipping wildly between images of Blake and grim foreboding about the interview to come. Her father was not going to like this marriage, chiefly because he had played no part in bringing it about. But for once she was not going to let them browbeat her. She was twenty-five, and it was time she made her own decisions.

The housekeeper admitted her to the vast hallway of her parents mock-Tudor home. Her mother was waiting in the formal living room, immaculately dressed, as always. Her gray hair was lacquered into rigid waves, her face expertly madé up to disguise any hint of natural imperfection. Kate dutifully kissed her mother's perfumed cheek, wishing that just once her mother would receive her clad in a rumpled housecoat with half its buttons missing. The thought was so ridiculous it made her smile. Her mother was no great believer in cozy informality.

"Well, Kate," she said, after making the usual polite inquiries about her daughter's drive out from the city, "I'm delighted to see you've returned to your senses at last and left that dreadful place you were staying. I never thought I'd see you—my own daughter—dressed in a dirty gingham blouse and a denim skirt." She uttered the word *denim* as if she were describing a faintly immoral fabric.

Kate twisted her hands nervously together. "I'd been cleaning house the day you arrived," she said. Her mother made no comment and Kate continued haltingly. "Actually, Mother, I haven't exactly left Windhaven. At least, I've left the farm, but I haven't left Blake."

"What do you mean?" her mother asked sharply.

Her mother's hostility was pointed enough to make Kate angry, and she forgot some of her nervousness. "I think it's obvious what I mean," she said. "I've come back to the city, but I'm not giving up my friendship with Blake. In fact—"

"I'm so glad you're back in Milwaukee," Mrs. Forsberg interrupted, speaking quickly, almost as if she was unwilling to let Kate finish her sentence for fear of what she might hear. "And, my dear, once you've introduced Blake to a few of your old friends, you'll never marry him. You were hysterical when you told us that. When I think of dear Steven . . . He was always so immaculately dressed, always the perfect gentleman."

Kate's anger boiled over. "Even when he was in bed

with another woman?" she asked. "Do you think Steven
was a perfect gentleman with all his mistresses? What's the
gentlemanly code for committing adultery, I wonder? Do
you just have to make sure your wife doesn't find out? Or
is there more to it?"

Mrs. Forsberg pressed an electric bell set into the wall
by the marble fireplace and remained silent until the housekeeper arrived. "We'll have some sherry," she said, tight-
lipped. As soon as they were alone again, she turned to face
her daughter. "I don't think this conversation is proving
very productive, Kate."

"No, it isn't. I'm sorry." Kate sat down on the silk-
quilted sofa, trying hard to suppress her resentment. She
changed the subject, hoping her mother's mood would im-
prove. "Is Dad coming home for lunch? I thought he might
if I called his secretary and let him know I'd be driving up."

"I expect he will, although he's especially busy at the
office these days. Steven's death came at a bad moment for
your father."

"Were Dad and Steven working on a business project
together?" Kate asked, surprised. "I didn't know that."

"There are a great many things you don't know," her
mother said, then clamped her lips together as the housekeeper entered the living room carrying a decanter of sherry
and two crystal glasses. But Kate had the distinct impression
the servant's entrance was merely an excuse rather than the
real reason for her mother's silence.

Kate sipped her sherry and tried to force herself to relax.
She was twenty-five, she kept reminding herself. There was
no way her mother could force her to give up Blake. She
experienced a wonderful feeling of release when she realized
her thoughts of self-reassurance were true. She wanted to
marry Blake, and her parents had no power to stop her. She
felt a moment of sympathy for her mother, who had never
known how to create bonds of love. Mrs. Forsberg was
discovering, to her cost, that threats and a sense of duty
could only push her daughter so far.

"I'm looking forward to seeing Dad," Kate said gently. "I heard a worrisome rumor the other day about his state of health. Does he know people are saying he's been ill? I can't imagine how the rumors started, but it must have a bad effect on Forsberg Industries if people keep spreading that sort of gossip."

Mrs. Forsberg turned gray under her makeup, and Kate got up, hurrying to her mother's side. "Mother, what is it? The rumors aren't true, are they? For heaven's sake, Dad isn't really sick is he?"

Some of her mother's color returned as she drained her glass of sherry. "Of course not," she said fiercely, not meeting Kate's eyes.

"Then what's the problem? Why were you so shattered when I reported something I'd thought was no more than a silly piece of gossip?"

"The economy is shaky and the lumber industry has been badly affected by the building slump. You should know enough about the business world to realize that Forsberg Industries can't afford to have rumors flying around the financial markets that its founder and president is too sick to do a proper job. He needs access to the loan markets, just as every other business does. Forsberg Industries is your father's life. Naturally I was upset when you told me what people are saying about your father's health." After a tiny pause, her mother added, "Who told you your father has been sick?"

"Betty Bergdorf mentioned it in passing. But Dad will be able to squash the stories now that he knows about them."

"Yes." Mrs. Forsberg sat down, recovering her poise. "It's amazing how these extraordinary tales leak out. Your father probably coughed twice when somebody blew cigar smoke in his face, and before you know it, rumor has him entering a TB sanitarium."

Kate was relieved to see that her mother was so quickly able to put the gossip in its proper perspective. "I wouldn't have mentioned it, except I wanted Dad to know what was being said." It certainly didn't seem appropriate to admit to her mother that she had wondered—just for a moment—if there might have been some substance to Betty's story.

The servant reentered the room to announce that a telephone message had been received from Mr. Forsberg's office. He couldn't make lunch, but he hoped to see Kate at dinner. "Lunch will be ready in fifteen minutes, Mrs. Forsberg," the housekeeper added.

"Time for another small sherry," Mrs. Forsberg said brightly. Her moment of panic seemed to have passed completely, and her control was as complete as ever. "Now, why did you drive up to see us today, Kate? When I heard you were coming, I must admit I hoped you'd had a change of heart about the trustee for Steven's estate. It's a terrible insult to your father if you don't allow him to administer the trust, you know."

"Mother, I've explained all this to you and Dad. As far as I'm concerned, Steven's money isn't morally mine. I can't allow *anybody* to administer it for my profit."

"So you're going ahead with that crazy idea of donating the money to charity?" Kate couldn't interpret the emotion behind her mother's question although, strangely enough, she didn't think it was anger.

"Yes," Kate replied mildly. "It's not as if I need the money, and I think Steven would appreciate what I'm doing on his behalf."

Her mother's expression remained unreadable behind its mask of makeup. "Then why did you come here today, Kate?" she asked after a short pause.

Kate took a deep breath. "I wanted to invite you and Dad to my wedding," she said. "Blake Koehler and I are getting married on Friday."

The silence stretched out for so long that Kate walked across the room to drop down on her knees beside her mother's chair. "Mother?" she said hesitantly. "Will you and Dad come to our wedding . . . please?"

Mrs. Forsberg pushed Kate's hand away from her arm as if it scalded her. She stood up, and her voice shook with rage. "You're really going to marry *that* man," she hissed. "I can't believe it! You've been a widow for less than three months! Steven was a member of one of the finest families in the state, and you plan to insult his memory by marrying Blake Koehler! Who is he, for heaven's sake? A nobody! An unemployed layabout who's after your money!"

Kate moved away from her mother. "I'm marrying Blake," she said quietly. "And I find your way of speaking about him offensive. You know he's not interested in my money. You and Dad discovered that when you tried to bribe him."

"What do you know about this man?" her mother continued, ignoring Kate's comment. "Just because he looks at you as though he can't wait to undress you, just because he can attract you physically, do you think that's any foundation for marriage?"

"It's a better foundation than your pride in his family tree," Kate replied bitterly. "Even if we have nothing else in common, at least we'll have fun in bed." She was horrified as soon as she had spoken, wishing she could recall the angry words. "That isn't what I meant, Mother. I do know something about Blake. You and Dad have the wrong impression. He isn't unemployed. In fact, we're leaving for Fiji the day after the wedding. Blake's working on a movie that's being filmed there."

"And I'm supposed to feel satisfied because you're marrying a man who'll have you trailing around the world after him to one God-forsaken spot after another? Fiji, for heaven's sake! Kate, have you gone out of your mind?"

"No," she said quietly. "I think I've just begun to find myself. I love Blake and he loves me. That's all we need to know about one another."

There was a light tap at the door. "Lunch is ready, Mrs. Forsberg," the servant announced.

"Thank you." Mrs. Forsberg looked coldly at her daughter. "Are you staying for lunch? Or do you want to rush back to your precious Blake?"

"Will you and Dad be able to attend the wedding?" Kate

persisted, not answering her mother's question directly. "I should like . . . Blake and I would like you to be there."

"No," said her mother. "I'm afraid your father and I have other plans for that day. I have no intention of lending my presence to something so disastrous. Just don't come crawling home to us when he leaves you penniless."

"Don't worry, I won't! I realize now that I should never have expected you to treat me like a daughter. As far as you and Dad are concerned, you didn't give birth to a baby. You simply produced a useful tool in Dad's corporate plans for development. I'm supposed to marry Dad's next takeover prospect, is that it? It certainly saves Dad an undignified public battle for shares! Unfortunately, I don't happen to relish the prospect of having a second husband who can't tell whether he has a wife in his bed or a division of Forsberg Lumber Company. Good-bye, Mother. I'm not in the mood for eating lunch."

Kate slammed out of the living room before her mother could see the tears of despair that filled her eyes and overflowed onto her cheeks. As she rushed along the huge hallway, she thought she heard the faint sound of her mother calling her name, but she refused to stop and listen. She wished Blake was waiting for her in the lonely Milwaukee apartment, to kiss her and hold her and reassure her that she was doing the right thing. But as she drove back to the city, she gradually became calmer. Her decision was irrevocable, she realized, and opposition from her mother had merely made her more determined to follow the instincts of her heart. All the background information in the world couldn't tell you whether a person was going to make a loving marriage partner. A computer would have declared that Kate and Steven were a perfect match. Which only went to show, she thought with a faint glimmer of humor, that computers and statistics were both liars. The memory of Blake's dark eyes, warm with laughter, rose up to blot out the image of her mother's rage and, with a little sigh of longing, she let herself into the empty apartment, comforted by the thought of Blake.

It was only late that night, as she drifted off into an uneasy sleep, that she began to question the violence of her mother's opposition to the match. Even for a strong-minded woman, thwarted in her wish to have an obedient daughter, her mother's rejection had been unexpectedly fierce. Why did she feel so threatened by the prospect of her daughter marrying Blake Koehler? That was the word, Kate thought drowsily. Her mother had seemed *threatened*.

As the mists of sleep finally claimed her, Kate recognized the emotion underlying all of her mother's angry outbursts. It had been fear, Kate realized. Stark, unrelieved fear.

- 7 -

IT WAS A pleasure to dress up for dinner with Blake, and
Kate was almost glad he had never before seen her in any
glamorous or sophisticated clothes. It was amazing, she
thought, as she touched lip gloss to her mouth, what an
expert haircut and some flattering makeup could do to im-
prove a woman's appearance.

She had spent the morning in a rush of organization,
making arrangements for the long-term garaging of her
Porsche and for the care of her apartment. She'd spent the
afternoon shopping and was pleased with the result of her
hours of searching. Her wedding dress, swathed in tissue,
hung in the closet. For this evening's date she had found
a simple dress of peacock green silk that contrasted with the
ethereal fairness of her hair and highlighted her green eyes.

She felt a shivering sense of anticipation as she sprayed

perfume against her neck, and her hands shook as she tried to put in her fragile gold hoop earrings. She was like a schoolgirl on her first date. But she knew the comparison was inaccurate. She was a woman, not a child, and her feelings for Blake had all the depth and intensity that only an adult could bring to a relationship. She had grown up since she'd met Blake, she thought as the earrings finally slipped into place. The knowledge was so pleasing that for a long time she stood motionless in front of her mirror, not seeing the elegant image it reflected.

Her reverie was interrupted by the ring of the doorbell, and she ran along the hall corridor to open the door, feeling breathless and absurdly shy.

She couldn't think of anything so say when she saw Blake standing impatiently in the outside hall. Tall and unbelievably handsome, he wore a dark suit of impeccable cut and fit. The whiteness of his crisp shirt gleamed against the tan of his skin, emphasizing the powerful thrust of his jaw and the unexpectedly classic perfection of his profile.

Blake eventually broke the lengthening silence. "Is this the apartment of Kate Danbury?" he asked with only the faintest quirk of a smile to belie the seriousness of his enquiry. "Or have I wandered by mistake into the home of Miss America?"

She laughed then, turning her face up eagerly to receive his kiss. "I was about to say something similar myself. Are you quite sure you're the casual Blake Koehler I've grown to know and love?"

He stepped into the hallway, all laughter fading from his dark gaze. "As long as you've learned to love me, that's all that matters," he said, and his voice was husky with emotion. He pulled her into his arms and kissed her thoroughly, his hands exploring her body in a restless, demanding rhythm.

He broke away from her at last. "Since we're all dressed up for the occasion, I guess we'd better go out and dazzle the town."

"I guess so."

"That dress of yours is certainly a knockout. Do you have *anything* on underneath?"

"Perhaps you'll find out later," she whispered, then turned hurriedly away, swept by a wave of shyness as she saw the flare of emotion in his eyes.

Blake's indrawn breath exploded in a sharp exclamation. "We'd better get out of here right now. You ought to remember I have two lonely nights of frustration taking their toll."

She pulled a wrap out of the hall closet, too excited to notice how Blake's eyes narrowed momentarily as he helped her drape the soft, creamy mink around her shoulders. She chattered all the way to the car, telling him of the little events of her day, avoiding, for the moment, the bad news of her parents' opposition to their marriage. By the time they reached Blake's rented car, warmth had returned to his expression.

He drove swiftly to the canopied entrance of Milwaukee's most celebrated restaurant.

"It's difficult to get a reservation here," Kate said doubtfully. "Did you call in advance?"

"It's all taken care of," he replied smoothly. She soon discovered Blake was perfectly correct in his assertion. They were conducted to a corner table, softly lighted and well away from the main crush of diners and equally removed from the waiters' route to the kitchen.

"What strings did you pull to get *this* prime table at such short notice?" she asked Blake with a little smile.

"I promised the maitre d' free tickets to the grand opening of my next movie," he said casually.

"Do stuntmen get free tickets?" Kate's voice registered her surprise. "Well, at least I know I'll be guaranteed a ringside view of all the latest action-packed thrillers."

"You don't go to the movies very much, do you Kate?"

"How did you guess that? But as a matter of fact, you're right. I've always enjoyed live theater, but I gave up going to movies when my dates stopped taking me to drive-ins."

"Any particular reason?"

"I guess four or five years of struggling for my virtue in the back seat of a car turned me off movies!"

"I'll have to see if I can turn you on again."

She smiled happily. "I look forward to having you teach me all the fine points of technique."

"Honey, don't set your sights too high. I'm just the stuntman."

She wasn't aware of any particular emphasis in his voice as he spoke, and she turned her attention to the menu. Blake selected their wine, and they sipped slowly as they talked.

It was just as it had been at Windhaven. Once they started talking, all the barriers between them seemed to melt away. He spoke easily and affectionately of his childhood and his erratic school career, where periods of brilliant academic success had been repeatedly interrupted by periods of prolonged recklessness. His parents, Kate learned, had been elderly when he was born, and she soon suspected they had been somewhat overwhelmed by the sheer dynamism of their energetic son.

"I think they were heartily relieved when I joined the merchant marine," he said. "That way they could boast to all their friends that I had a respectable job, and they never had to inquire too deeply about what mischief I might get up to when my ship was in port."

"Did you get into mischief?" Kate asked with a twinkle in her eye.

"Not really." His eyes displayed an answering gleam. With an abrupt change of subject, he rested his hand over hers. "Tell me about your work at the Center. What did the Principal say when you told her you had to resign?"

Kate repeated much of her conversation with Mrs. Kearney, making sure she created the impression that the money being given to the Center was being donated under the terms of Steven's will. She didn't want to explain to Blake how unjustified she felt in taking her husband's money. Her first marriage was still a subject she preferred not to discuss with anybody.

"Is it a real problem for the Center that you're leaving so unexpectedly?" Blake asked.

"It is unless Steven's money is released quickly," Kate said. "The Center has no funds to hire a replacement teacher for me. Do you know anything about autistic children, Blake?"

"Not much."

"It's still something of a mysterious condition. It's difficult to diagnose with certainty, and doctors disagree as to its precise cause. But over the past ten years or so various specialists have found out how they can work together to help alleviate the symptoms. We still don't know what causes the problems, but at last we seem to be having real success in treating some cases. However, it requires endless patience on the part of the teacher and, at crucial stages in the education process, the children have to be worked with on an individual basis." For a moment, worry clouded the happiness in her face. "I feel very guilty," she said. "Leaving the Center without proper notice is just about the only cloud on my horizon."

"Can't parents volunteer to help?"

"Not always. Autistic children refuse to acknowledge the existence of people around them, which is hard for parents to accept. The children sit for hours in a corner, rocking themselves back and forth, flapping their hands wildly if they get agitated. Sometimes they start to beat their heads against the wall, seemingly for no reason. Most mothers and fathers can only take small doses of watching their tiny children bang their heads on solid brick walls. Of course, it tears the teachers apart as well, but at least we're trained, and we aren't watching our own children."

"It seems a very worthwhile job you've been doing, Kate. But I'm selfish enough not to volunteer to delay our marriage until the Center finds a replacement. I need you too much."

"And I need you," she replied softly.

The waiter arrived with their main course, interrupting a moment of almost tangible awareness. When they were alone again, Blake made a visible effort to reduce the level of emotional tension by asking how Mr. and Mrs. Forsberg had reacted to the news of their daughter's imminent marriage.

"Not well," Kate acknowledged.

Blake's gaze was sympathetic. "Was it very bad?" he asked quietly.

"Yes, I guess you could say it was pretty grim. My mother . . . thinks I'm a fool."

"Are your parents going to come to the wedding, even though they disapprove?"

"No." She dropped her gaze, saddened by the admission.

His strong fingers curled around her hand, comforting her. "There are only two people who matter at a marriage ceremony," he said softly. "And we'll both be there."

She was grateful for his intuitive sensitivity, and she managed a faint smile. "At least if you jilt me at the altar, there'll be nobody there to witness my disgrace!"

"No fear of that. I'm definitely not planning to let you get away from me!" Blake's expression turned thoughtful. "Did your father seem quite well to you, Kate, when you went to give your parents the news?"

"Have you heard those strange rumors, too?" she asked quickly. "Who told you he was ill?"

"I had to see the local bank manager and the local realtor when I put the farm on the market. I mentioned that I was marrying you, and they both asked if it was true that Forsberg Industries was having some sort of financial crisis. They were very vague, but they said gossip was rife that your father had had a heart attack."

"That's nonsense!" Kate exclaimed. "You know it is! You saw him yourself when he came to Windhaven." She was relieved to be able to be so dogmatic in her denial. While her father might have some minor ailment, he couldn't have suffered a heart attack without her knowing it. She frowned. "It's dreadful the way people take every scrap of information about public figures and twist it into some totally false story."

She didn't understand the bitterness of Blake's laughter. "You're right there," he agreed. "Well, I'm glad the rumors about your father are false. We can take off for Fiji with a clear conscience."

"I can't believe we're getting married tomorrow." Kate gazed into Blake's dark eyes, hovering between panic and excitement. "Forty-eight hours from now we'll be on a Pacific Island. I'll be Mrs. Koehler!"

Blake's grip tightened around her fingers. "Let's get out of here." He flung down a wad of money without waiting for the check, and hurried her into his rented car. He drove in silence to a deserted spot close to Lake Michigan, where he parked the car and asked her if she would come for a walk.

They strolled hand in hand to the water's edge, staring silently into the dark waves. The night air carried the chill sting of September in its breath, and Kate shivered slightly despite her wrap.

"Lean against me," Blake murmured. "I'll keep you warm."

She turned slowly in his arms, speaking before she had a chance to think. "I love you, Blake." She was shattered to hear herself making the admission. She felt exposed, vulnerable, because she had let him see the truth about her innermost feelings.

He kissed her mouth with exquisite tenderness. "I nearly forgot to give you this," he said. He drew a small box from his pocket, and she opened it to find an old-fashioned gold engagement ring, set with six tiny emeralds in the shape of a flower. She said nothing, because the lump in her throat made speech impossible.

"I'll understand if you don't want to take off Steven's rings," Blake said quietly. "Perhaps you could wear this on your right hand until you get used to the idea that I'm going to be your husband."

Silently she drew off Steven's diamond ring and the fashionable platinum wedding band that matched it. She held out her hand to Blake. "Please put your ring on," she said.

He slipped it on her finger. "The emeralds match your eyes," he said gruffly. "The ring belonged to my mother, but I'll buy you something more elaborate later on."

"Please don't. Nothing could be better than this."

"I'll drive you home. It's getting late." When they drew up outside her apartment building, he stood with her on the sidewalk, making no move to come up with her.

"I've decided to spend the night in my hotel. I've left my luggage there, and I don't want to have to rush around tomorrow morning getting back to the hotel in time to change." There was a trace of color darkening the tan of his cheeks, and Kate was certain he was lying.

"That's not the real reason you don't want to stay with me."

He shuffled his feet uncomfortably. "If you must know, I'm superstitious, damn it! It's bad luck to see your bride the night before you marry."

"In that case, we've already blown it," she said teasingly. Secretly, her heart was almost bursting with love at this unexpected confession. "All right, Blake," she said. "I'll try to hold my wicked passions in check until tomorrow night."

He kissed her roughly and turned to go.

"Blake!" she called him back.

"What is it?"

"When and where are we getting married?"

"I'm sorry . . . I forgot. We'll be married in Judge Ashton's chambers at eleven A.M. Main courthouse building."

"Blake!" She called him back again. "How am I supposed to get there? Shall I take a cab?"

"If you wouldn't mind. There are still a couple of business matters I need to take care of tomorrow morning." He smiled ruefully. "I'm not being very efficient, am I?"

"You just forgot a few trivial details," Kate said, trying unsuccessfully to hide her affectionate laughter. "Any man could forget to let his wife-to-be know where they're going to be married."

He scowled at her with mock ferocity. "Wait until tomorrow night when I'm not feeling so nervous," he said through clenched teeth. "I'll teach you proper respect for your lord and master!"

"I look forward to the lessons," she said huskily.

He turned abruptly and the moonlight caught his dark hair, turning the blackness to silver and etching his features into sharp relief. Kate caught her breath, both at the devastating sensuality of his appearance and at the haunting impression of familiarity that gripped her. It was the third time, she realized, that she had been overwhelmed by this strange feeling of having known Blake Koehler before.

He waved his hand in a final farewell before disappearing into the darkness of the car's interior, and she walked slowly into the lobby of her apartment building. She tried to shake the uncomfortable sensations away as she rode up in the elevator. It was pre-wedding nerves, she told herself. She had never even visited Los Angeles. There was no way she could ever have met Blake Koehler before. He wasn't exactly a man it would be easy to forget, she told herself with a faint smile.

The memory of his kiss lingered on her lips as she prepared for bed, and her dreams remained untroubled by any premonition of disaster.

She was amazed at how calm she felt as she put on the pale pink dress she had chosen for their wedding. She fastened the row of tiny buttons with steady fingers, confident as she had never been before, that she was doing exactly the right thing.

She smoothed her long hair into a chignon, softening the

severity of the style with delicate filigree earrings. The pink of her dress, so pale that in some lights the silk looked cream rather than pink, reflected soft color into her face, enhancing the natural bloom of her complexion.

The doorbell rang, warning her that the taxi had arrived. She cast one final look around the bedroom she had occupied in solitary splendor for the last two years of her marriage to Steven. She was glad to be leaving it. Her suitcases, three matched pieces bearing a designer label, lay by her dressing table waiting to be picked up en route to the airport. She took a deep breath. She was ready to go.

Blake was waiting on the courthouse steps, slightly pale beneath his tan. If possible, he looked even more handsome than he had the previous night, dressed in a gray mohair suit cut to emphasize the superb condition of his body. She was suddenly shy as she got out of the cab and almost wished she had an old-fashioned bridal veil to draw across her face.

"Good luck, miss," the cab driver said. "You sure do make a beautiful bride." He spotted Blake hurrying toward them and gave a gasp. "Is *that* who you're marrying, miss?"

"Yes." She was so happy to see Blake, she scarcely heard what the driver was saying. She smiled tremulously as he arrived at her side. "Hello," she greeted him softly.

He raised her hand to his lips and dropped a kiss into her palm. "I didn't think anybody could look more beautiful than you did last night, but you've proven me wrong."

"You like my dress?"

"It's perfect," he said simply. He noticed the cab driver, still staring at them with an expression of overwhelming astonishment, and he quickly pressed a folded bill into the man's hand. "This is a *private* ceremony," he said, his voice hard. "Understand, friend?"

"Sure, sure. You mean nobody knows?"

"And that's the way I want to keep it." Blake put his arm around Kate and hurried her into the courthouse building. "We'd better be punctual or the judge will take off for lunch."

"At eleven in the morning?" Kate asked, laughing because today everything seemed to add to her happiness. Even the cab driver's strange amazement seemed comical when she thought back on it.

"The legal profession takes long lunch hours," Blake muttered.

Judge Ashton, however, was waiting patiently in his office when they arrived. He looked solemn and dignified, well aware of the authority of his office. There was no doubt, Kate thought as she listened to his sonorous voice, that a couple united by Judge Ashton would feel well and truly married. She began to shake a little, all her earlier confidence evaporating under Judge Ashton's severe gaze. Marriage, he pointed out sternly, was not a step to be undertaken lightly. Nervously, Kate assured him that she had thought very seriously about what she was doing.

The next few moments passed by Kate in a blurred murmur of voices. But when Blake slipped the narrow gold ring on her finger, she risked a glance up and felt her heart contract with love at the emotions she read in the depths of his dark eyes.

She signed the marriage certificates in a haze of happiness, only returning to earth when Blake escorted her out of the judge's chambers and kissed her thoroughly. "Do you feel married, Mrs. Koehler?" he asked her teasingly.

"Not yet," she breathed. "I need some more convincing."

He kissed her again, then drew her hand through his arm. "I can think of better places to continue this exercise than a drafty courthouse corridor. Let's pick up your luggage and start the drive to Chicago. Do you think if we hang a DO NOT DISTURB sign on our hotel door at three in the afternoon, they'll guess we're honeymooners?"

She laughed. "Maybe we can pretend we're long-distance air travelers, switching time zones. Three o'clock in Chicago must be midnight somewhere in the world."

He dropped a kiss on the tip of her nose. "Mrs. Koehler, you have brains as well as beauty. You're a jewel among wives."

"Do you realize we've been married for thirteen minutes, and we haven't exchanged a cross word?"

"Compatability could go no further." He smiled as he responded to her nonsense. "We can go out of the main entrance. My car's parked just across the street."

They emerged from the gloom of the courthouse interior into brilliant fall sunshine. For a moment Kate was too dazzled by the light to see anything clearly. Then her astonished gaze fell on a television minicam crew. A reporter with a microphone turned swiftly as they stepped out of the door and hurried purposefully toward them.

Kate glanced over her shoulder, wondering if somebody important was emerging from the courthouse behind her. To her bewilderment, the doorway and the steps were deserted.

"Hell and damnation," Blake said, and Kate stared at him in puzzlement. "I should've known that damn cab driver would spread the word," he added.

"Blake, what do you mean?" Her eyes darkened with apprehension as she questioned him. "What is it, Blake? What do they want?"

He held her more tightly against his side. "Forgive me, Kate, I should have told you before. There's no time now." With an expression almost of weariness, he turned to face the camera crew. "I suppose it's useless asking you to leave us alone?" he called out.

The cameramen didn't answer, but the reporter reached them at that moment, panting slightly as he extended the microphone toward Blake. "I'm Mike Warren, reporter-at-large for WRN news. How does it feel to be a married man at last, Mr. Harrington?"

"It would feel better if I weren't surrounded by camera crews," Blake said, his voice resigned rather than angry.

A small crowd, materializing out of nowhere at the sight

of the television news team, began to press closer to the threesome on the courthouse steps. "It's Blake Harrington," Kate heard somebody say. Blake Harrington... Blake Harrington... The name rippled through the crowd in a wave of rising excitement.

Mike Warren laughed jovially. "You've certainly found a beautiful bride, Mr. Harrington. Where and when did you two meet?"

Kate didn't hear Blake's reply. She was glad he was holding her tightly against the rock-hardness of his body; otherwise she was afraid she might have fallen. Blake *Harrington?* She stared at him with eyes blinded by shock, but after a few seconds the mists cleared and, when she could see again, she wondered how she had been deceived—even for a minute, let alone for weeks. The man she was leaning against, clutching onto for support—the man she had just married with all the legality the state of Wisconsin could provide—was Blake Harrington. The superstar who four years ago had exploded onto the world's movie screens with a space adventure movie that had broken all box office records. Last year's sequel, defying the gloomy predictions of the film industry, had surpassed the success of the original. Her whole body began to shake, and her face turned white. Why had he deceived her like this?

"Blake?" she said, not bothering that the reporter was in the middle of another question. "Blake..." she said again, and then she couldn't find any way to phrase her questions. The shock seemed to have numbed her thought processes.

"I'm sorry, Kate. I didn't want it to be this way."

The reporter misinterpreted Blake's words. "If you'll please give your husband a kiss, Mrs. Harrington, I'll be able to call the camera crew off. What does it feel like to be kissed by the man who was voted Hollywood's sexiest male star?"

"It feels fine... er... fine," she responded mechanically.

"We'd better get this over with. Then they may leave us alone," Blake said as he turned her around in his arms. He bent and kissed her swiftly on the lips. Her mouth felt colder than a block of ice, and she wondered if he could feel her teeth chattering. It seemed as though they must be visibly knocking together.

Mike Warren evidently found the strange kiss perfectly satisfactory. True to his word, he signaled to the camera crew to stop filming as soon as Blake drew away from Kate's lips. "Show's over, folks," he called to the crowd. "I appreciated the interview, Mr. and Mrs. Harrington," he continued in a lower voice. "I'll ask the guys to hold back the crowd so you don't get swamped by autograph hunters." He held out his hand to Kate and shook her limp fingers firmly. "I surely appreciated that exclusive tip from you, Mrs. Harrington. Our channel is going to have the scoop of the month on its news program tonight! Nobody else had heard a word about your marriage, and our managing director has asked me to thank you personally. We appreciate your decision to let our station be the first to know about your wedding plans. Thanks again, Mrs. Harrington." He raised his hand in a semi-salute to Blake. "And thanks to you for the interview, Mr. Harrington. There sure are going to be a lot of disappointed ladies watching our newscast tonight."

Blake's hold on Kate's waist had tightened convulsively as Mike Warren was speaking, and he acknowledged the man's effusive thanks with the briefest of nods. Kate tried to smile at the reporter, although she was too dazed to think about the significance of his words. She stole another glance at Blake's averted head, still trying to explain to herself how she had failed to recognize him. She was hurt to discover that Blake's features had frozen suddenly into a mask of black, angry isolation.

He turned to her as soon as Mike Warren was gone, running his eyes scornfully over her bewildered features. His mouth tightened into a grim line of dislike.

"You can cut the cute, bewildered act, honey. Your friend Mike has gone, and surely you don't think I'd be sucker enough to fall for it twice?"

A group of giggling, middle-aged housewives dodged around the camera crew and pressed close to Blake, making it unnecessary for Kate to find a reply.

"Mr. Harrington, could we have your autograph, please?" One woman, bolder than the rest, thrust forward a shopping list, and Blake smiled charmingly as he scrawled his name across the paper. He repeated the process several times, his smile never fading.

"We wish you both every happiness, Mr. Harrington," another of the women called out as he finally started to move away, hustling Kate with him.

"Thank you. I think it's guaranteed." He raised Kate's hand to his lips, and a concerted sigh of pleasure rose from the onlookers as he appeared to kiss the tips of her fingers.

And she'd never guessed he was an actor, Kate thought bitterly. His mask of charm dropped as soon as they were out of sight of the crowd.

"Get in the car," he ordered tersely.

Anger finally dispersed some of her numbness. "What have I done?" she asked. "Why are you behaving this way, Blake? I'm not the one who married you under false pretenses. It's the other way around, remember?"

"I said to get in the car. I'm an actor, Kate, and I'm up on all the tricks in your book. Outraged innocence isn't going to work any better than tears of bewilderment."

"I don't know what you mean—"

"Save it, honey." He glanced at his watch. "It's only twelve thirty," he said with a harsh laugh. "I feel I've lived a lifetime in the last half hour."

"Don't we all," Kate said, not bothering to conceal her bitterness.

"Don't complain, honey. We were happily married for the first thirteen minutes. For a Hollywood marriage, I guess that wasn't too bad."

- 8 -

BLAKE DROVE IN forbidding silence all the way to Chicago's
O'Hare Airport. He swerved the car sharply into a space
in the parking lot of the Hyatt Regency Hotel, and the squeal
of the tires was the loudest noise Kate had heard since she
got into the car.

The check-in at the hotel proceeded with complete
smoothness. The porters and the desk clerk didn't recognize
Blake, but they responded unhesitatingly to his inherent air
of command. How had she missed it? Kate asked herself
despairingly. How could she have spent so many hours with
him in public places and not realized he had the total as-
surance that only comes to a truly successful man? She
would not . . . could not . . . think about the more frightening
problem hovering at the back of her mind. Why was Blake
so angry with her? What had she done to deserve such icy
fury?

The elevator carried them to a suite on the top floor of the hotel. The porter disposed of their luggage on the special racks and gestured to a low table in the sitting room.

"The champagne you ordered is on ice, sir," he said.

"Thank you." Blake handed the man a generous tip as he left the room, then walked quickly to the bucket of champagne. He ripped off the foil and packaging wire from the top of the bottle and pushed the cork out with a carelessness that caused champagne to froth out all over his sleeve. He poured the bubbling liquid into the two tall stemmed glasses and held one out to Kate with a mocking gesture. He ignored the spreading damp patch on his jacket.

"Let's make a toast," he said. "To Mrs. Harrington, who must be one of the smartest cookies in the business."

Kate's hand shook as she accepted the glass. She swallowed the champagne in a single, defiant gulp. "Would you care to explain that remark?" she asked. She was careful to keep her voice low and controlled. If she started to shout, she might never be able to stop.

"What would you like me to explain?" he asked jeeringly. "How I allowed myself to be taken in by some of the oldest tricks of the trade? Or would you prefer that I describe how I spent so much time gazing into your green eyes that I forgot to see the trickery flashing at the back of them?"

She looked at him steadily. "You knew who *I* was, Blake. I never lied to you about my past. But you've been lying to me about yourself ever since we met. Why are *you* shouting at *me?* Surely I'm the one who ought to be angry, if either of us should?"

He poured another glass of champagne, swallowing it in quick, nervous gulps. "God, Kate, but you're good. Did I once tell you you couldn't act? Forget what I said . . . You're a mistress of the art. What the hell do you mean: You're the one who ought to be angry? Do you think I'm so crazy about you that I don't even care how you set me up?"

"Are you suggesting that I knew all along who you really were? That I turned up at Windhaven just to try and trap you into some sort of permanent relationship? Is that what you're accusing me of?"

"That's it, sugar baby. You've got it in one."

"You're crazy. How could I have known you were at the farm?"

He shrugged. "It's just possible your arrival at Windhaven was a lucky chance. But you certainly seized your opportunity as soon as you recognized me. Amnesia! My God, you pulled the oldest trick there is, and I fell for it!"

"What reason do you have for assuming I recognized you?"

Blake pretended to think. "Let me see, what exactly did our friend the TV reporter say? I think it was something along these lines: 'Thank you, Mrs. Harrington for the exclusive tipoff. We appreciate the fact that you wanted our station to be the first to know.'" Blake mimicked the reporter's intonation with devastating accuracy. "Only you and I knew when and where we were getting married," he said. "And I sure as hell wasn't the one who called WRN news."

"Neither was I," she said quietly.

He laughed gratingly. "Try pulling the other leg, honey."

"You mean, despite all the time we've spent together ... the things we've promised to each other ... you're prepared to throw all that away because of some chance remark by a TV newsman? If I'd known who you really were, do you think I'd have been mad enough to risk setting up TV coverage for our wedding?"

"A woman who deliberately sets out to associate with a movie star must want publicity. Otherwise, why pick on a celebrity? Do you have any idea how many women are hung up on my phony image? The larger-than-life Blake Harrington who's projected onto a giant screen in glorious technicolor? Can you guess how many letters the studio receives from young girls who are willing to promise me *anything* if I'll allow my name to be linked with theirs? Is that what attracted you to me, Kate? Are you one of the women who can't separate an actor from the parts he plays? Are you turned on by all that celluloid sex and violence?"

"No, I'm not," she said, but she felt so weary she guessed her voice lacked conviction. She wondered bitterly where all her earlier certainties had vanished to. She had thought that this time she was marrying a man she could trust with her love forever. Now it seemed she had married a man she scarcely knew. Everything about him—his name, his profession, the anger of his rejection—all this belonged to a man she felt she had never met. She was sharing the honeymoon suite with a stranger.

"I'm tired, Blake," she said, turning away from the accusation lingering in his eyes. "I think I'll take a shower."

"Nothing more to say in your own defense, Kate? My, my, you are giving up easily." He gulped down the final dregs of the champagne. "I suppose I have one thing to congratulate myself on. At least I can be reasonably confident that you aren't marrying me for my money."

"That must be a great comfort to you," she said, and the pain he had inflicted tinged her words with acid.

There was a sudden silence in the room, and Kate, her mind still reeling under the stress of so many shocks and so much anger, stood awkwardly, uncertain of what to do or say next. She could feel Blake's eyes examining her intently, stripping away all her layers of protection. She dropped her gaze, wanting to hide her emotions from his ruthless examination, and she heard his breath draw in with a little hiss.

"So that's it," he breathed and his voice was tight with self-mockery. He laughed again, the sound jarring Kate's lacerated nerves. "And to think I spent all that time at Windhaven congratulating myself on the fact that *at last* I'd found a woman who couldn't possibly care about my money!"

"What are you talking about, Blake?"

"Steven left all his money to charity, you told me so yourself," Blake said slowly. "And your father's been ill, so the rumors say. . . . I wonder what I would discover if I ran a financial check on the current condition of Forsberg Industries? Do you think I'd find that the company is in its former state of robust health, Kate? Or might I find that your source of income is wasting away to the point of vanishing? A young woman like yourself, who keeps her hall closet stuffed casually full of mink wraps, might not like the thought of a future uncushioned by her Daddy's money. And with Steven gone . . . Yes, I can see that another rich husband would be pretty essential."

Kate felt physically sick. "Your mind's been warped by the studio's publicity," she said. "For God's sake, don't you think anybody sees you as a man? Do you imagine everybody sees you either as a sex symbol or as a bank account?"

"Honey, ninety-nine percent of the time, I'm sure of it. One percent of the time, there's a little room for doubt."

"Make your financial check on Forsberg Industries, Blake. If the success of our marriage hangs on the chance words of a TV newscaster and the report of a financial analyst, then it was scarcely worth calling it a marriage in the first place." Blake was so determined to believe what he wanted to believe that she didn't even bother to tell him her money was now invested in Steven's family business rather than her parents'. She turned to leave the room, but Blake put out his hand and pulled her roughly toward the phone.

"Oh, no you don't, sweetie. You can stay and listen to every word of this."

She deliberately tried to make her mind a blank while he placed his call to one of the major brokerage houses in New York. However, she couldn't help hearing that he was on first-name terms with the president and senior partner. Why not? she thought with a cynicism that was new to her. He could probably buy out the company if he wanted to. It paid the president to be all willingness to please.

Blake put the phone back in its cradle and walked away from Kate to the tiny refrigerator, set into a small bar in one corner of the room. He swung open the door and extracted two miniature bottles of Scotch and a tray of ice cubes. "Care to join me while I wait for the return call?" he said to Kate, gesturing with false courtesy toward the bottles.

"No, thank you."

"Tut, tut, Kate, don't let your bad temper show. You'll never get a big fat alimony settlement if you aren't nice to me. In fact, if you want any alimony at all, I'll expect you to be *very* nice. All the time."

She was overcome by a sense of frustration that was so strong she wanted to scream. "Blake," she pleaded, not quite brave enough to touch him, "this is insane! Why are you doing this to me? A few words from a man neither of us knew, and we're twisting our whole lives into a disaster. Blake . . . please . . . You know you don't really believe what you're saying."

The glass of whiskey halted halfway to his mouth, and Kate held her breath. She had got through to him at last! He took a tentative step in her direction, then the telephone shrilled into the silence of the room. The whiskey sloshed in his glass, showing he was not nearly as cool as he wanted to pretend. He strode grimly to the phone and snatched up the receiver. "Harrington here," he said curtly.

She watched him in growing despair. He said very little but gradually his face set into lines of bitterness and self-derision. "Thank you, Ted," he said just before replacing the phone. "That's more or less what I expected to hear."

Kate looked at him. She guessed that her face was drained of all color, but she wasn't going to give him the satisfaction of breaking down in front of him.

"How was the report on Forsberg Industries?" she asked, proud that she managed to keep her voice steady.

"Bad," Blake said succinctly. "But then that's no surprise to you, is it honey bun?" She cringed at his repeated use of false endearments, but forced herself to meet his eyes.

"It *is* a surprise," she contradicted him. "But not as big a one as finding out that I'd married Blake Harrington."

"For your information—as if you didn't know already—

Forsbert Industries is critically short of cash. It's the opinion of industry analysts that the company is overextended and undermanaged. It's borrowed heavily and is being bled to death by the high interest rates it has to pay. No wonder you were running scared, honey."

She lifted her head proudly. "My personal income isn't dependent on Forsberg Industries." She refused to give him any further explanation. If he could misunderstand her so completely, why should she tell him that her private fortune had all been taken out of Forsberg Industries and converted to stock in Steven's family company at the time of her first marriage.

"You mean, you *hope* your personal income isn't dependent on Forsberg Industries. What have you got to offer me in exchange, if I volunteer to keep you in the luxury to which you've always been accustomed?"

"Nothing," she said. "Do you want a divorce?"

"Oh, no," he said. "I've waited thirty-five years to get married, so I think I'd like to savor the delights of marital bliss for a bit longer than four or five hours. At the very least, my experience with you should serve as a warning for the future. Don't you agree, my dear Mrs. Harrington?"

"I don't know," she said. "Some people never seem to acquire any sense where falling in love is concerned."

"My, my, that's another very bitter statement from a young woman who still has most of her life in front of her. Third time lucky, you know, Kate my sweet."

She could no longer hold in check the tears blurring her eyes, and they spilled out through her lashes, running on to her cheeks. She would not admit to their existence by wiping them away, and she stood in the middle of the room, staring blindly ahead of her.

Suddenly Blake seized her arm, shaking her. "Stop it, do you hear? I said stop it!" Angrily, he pulled a handkerchief from his jacket pocket and rubbed it roughly across her wet cheeks.

"Damn it, Kate, you have most professional actresses

beaten hollow. First you deceive me with your brilliant performance as a sensitive young woman, crushed by bullying parents. Now you actually have me feeling guilty because I've told you a few home truths."

She concentrated on holding back her tears. "I don't think this conversation is leading anywhere, Blake. Do you want me to leave?"

"And have Sacha and Joni and the rest of the movie team pestering me with questions as soon as I arrive in Fiji? No, I don't want you to leave right at the moment."

"Do you want a divorce as soon as we get back from Fiji?"

"No," he said curtly. "I don't want a divorce. I've spent the past five years having every action I take examined under a microscope by the popular press. I have no intention of handing the scandal sheets a front-page story about Blake Harrington's four-week marriage. You're going to stay with me, Kate, and look as though you're enjoying every minute."

"Why should I? Why should I choose to be humiliated by you?"

"Because courts don't award alimony to wives who've stayed with their husbands less than a month. If you want to get the settlement you set your mercenary heart on, you'd better stay with me as long as I'm prepared to keep you. Who knows? If you're a good girl, after four or five years I might forget why you married me."

"You've misunderstood everything, Blake. You don't begin to understand why I married you."

"Tell me again it's because you love me. You did that so beautifully last night: the soft voice, the downcast eyes. It was absolutely perfect."

She recoiled from the mockery in his voice. "Don't, Blake . . . please."

"Honey," he said, "it's obvious why you married me. You wanted to lead the glamorous life of Mrs. Blake Harrington. Your income was shrinking. Perhaps you decided

Milwaukee was too small a city to do justice to your spectacular talents. Well, I fell for your scheming, and I'll go along with the consequences. I'm prepared to give you the whole world to play in, and my bank account is at your disposal for as long as you remain with me. There's only one thing that's not included in the deal: You can have my name, my house, my cars, my money, but just remember, Kate, that you'll never have me."

She could think of nothing to say in reply to his bitter accusations. She wanted to collapse on the bed and cry until there were no tears left, but she would not expose her vulnerability to him ever again. God knew, her years with Steven had taught her how to hide her emotional hurts.

She managed to look at him without tears. "Have you said all you want to say? If so, I'd like to take a bath."

"What else is left to say?" Blake asked, and Kate felt her heart contract at the raw emotion in his voice. But his pain—if it had ever been there—was hidden again in less than a second. "Take your bath, *Mrs. Harrington*. You can spend all night in the bathroom as far as I'm concerned. I'm going out to look for more congenial company."

She wouldn't let him see how his words affected her. Not women, she thought. Please don't let it be another woman. She couldn't stand that humiliation again. She walked unseeingly toward the bathroom.

"Kate!" His harsh call stopped her at the door. "Be ready tomorrow morning at eight. We have to catch a plane at ten-fifteen and we shouldn't miss it. I don't want to hang around in Chicago all day, waiting for the next direct flight."

"I'll be ready," she said stonily. Please go, she thought. Please let me get into the bathroom before I break up completely.

"Make yourself beautiful tomorrow, sweetie pie. We want to be sure you don't ruin my image. My fans like to think I have the pick of the world's luscious ladies."

She gathered herself together for one last burst of defiance. "I'll take care not to hurt your image, Blake, because

I realize it's all you've got. If there was a real man underneath that macho image you're projecting, you'd stop shouting long enough to find out if what you're saying is true. Enjoy your night out." She slammed the door of the bathroom shut, ramming the bolt into its lock before slumping against the wall in a state of collapse.

It was a luxurious bathroom, much larger than the average hotel room, and there was a floor-to-ceiling mirror attached to one wall. She stared at the woman reflected in the glass. The pale pink dress, every bit as elegant as it had been when she put it on that morning, shimmered in the fluorescent light. Her hair was still smoothly clustered at the nape of her neck. Her face was pale, but her tears hadn't disturbed any mascara. "You look pretty much all in one piece," she told her reflection, then laughed with a tinge of hysteria. Even the mirror was a liar today. Why didn't it reflect a Kate who felt shattered into a hundred painful fragments?

She took a long bath, scrubbing at her skin as if to erase every trace of bitter memory. She ate an apple from a bowl of fruit, then slipped into her midnight-blue satin nightgown. What was the point of getting dressed? She refused to remember the pleasure she had felt in buying the nightgown. She had imagined the light in Blake's eyes when he saw the provocative slit in the side, the froth of lace at the plunging neckline.

She walked into the sitting room and placed a call to her parents. She felt a million miles away from Forsberg Industries and its problems, but she knew she ought to telephone and see if there was anything she could do to help. The housekeeper told her Mr. and Mrs. Forsberg were in New York. "No message," Kate said as she replaced the phone. At least it was further proof that her father was not ill. Her parents wouldn't be traveling thousands of miles if her father's health wasn't good.

Kate shivered as she walked into the bedroom and saw the huge, king-sized bed, its covers turned back on either side, inviting two newlyweds to enjoy making love in its welcoming embrace. Defiantly, she stretched herself across the middle of the huge bed and listened to the distant roar of a plane taking off from O'Hare. She would not think of the fact that her body scarcely made a dent in the vast expanse of sheets and blankets. She switched off all the lights, because in the darkness it was easier to forget that she would be sleeping here alone.

She stared, dry-eyed, into the comforting blackness. Why was she doing this? Why was she lying there, inviting Blake to humiliate her? Why didn't she simply get up and walk away?

She tossed and turned, trying not to discover the answer to her own questions, but even the darkness could not disguise the truth for long. Despite all he had done, despite his angry rejection, she still loved Blake. It was better to be miserable with him in Fiji than to be left, less than half-alive, in the cold familiarity of her Milwaukee apartment.

It was almost dawn before she heard a stumble of feet in the sitting room, and the muffled sound of Blake's curses as he righted some fallen piece of furniture. He blundered into the bedroom, making no effort to keep quiet, but she feigned sleep as he stood by the bed, staring down at her. Even at that distance she could smell the fumes of alcohol drifting from his body.

After a long time, he turned and made his way quietly out of the room. In a few moments, she heard the bathroom door slam shut.

She opened her eyes and lay against the pillows, watching the sun brighten behind the closed drapes. It was the second day of their marriage. With a shudder of pain, she acknowledged to herself that, in spite of everything, she wished—achingly and yearningly—that she had not spent her wedding night alone.

- 9 -

KATE WAS EXHAUSTED when the plane touched down at
Nandi Airport. The long hours of flying would have been
tiring in any circumstances, but her weariness was exac-
erbated by the subtle cruelty of Blake's behavior.

They had been seated in the first-class cabin of the 747
jet and, because there were few other passengers, the stew-
ardesses had plenty of time to be attentive. Before many
minutes of the journey had elapsed, it became obvious that
word was flashing round the cabin crew that "Mr. and Mrs.
Koehler" were actually Blake Harrington and his bride.

A young stewardess, blushing and smiling prettily,
paused by their seat with a bottle of champagne resting in
a bucket of ice.

"With the Captain's compliments, Mr. Harrington. He's delighted you chose to fly our airline."

"Thank you." Blake's answering smile was a miracle of warmth and charm, and Kate was astonished to feel his arm drop casually around her shoulders. It was the first time he had voluntarily touched her since their encounter with the TV news reporter. He spoke again to the stewardess.

"I guess you won't believe me if I try to tell you my name is Blake Koehler?" The quizzical grin that accompanied his words was attractive enough to coax even Queen Victoria into a small smile. The stewardess was completely won over. She gave a shy, breathless little laugh.

"Oh, Mr. Harrington, you're teasing! As if anybody could ever meet you in person and not recognize you instantly!"

Blake's hand tightened against Kate's shoulder, but his voice and smile remained bland. "What do you think of that, darling? Do you think we'll manage to spend any time alone? I know how much you were hoping nobody would recognize me."

His fingers pressed sharply through the thin cotton of Kate's dress, but pride prevented her from uttering even a small cry of pain. "Was I?" she asked, refusing to participate in his game. Her throat was so dry with tension that the words came out in a hoarse whisper.

"Darling, you're still exhausted from last night. . . ." His deliberately suggestive murmur could easily be heard by the stewardess. "Let me see if I can revive you. . . ." He leaned across the seat and brushed a kiss against her cheek. Kate trembled, hating herself for betraying any response at all to the cold, cynical flick of Blake's tongue against her skin.

"We saw you and your husband on the news last night, Mrs. Harrington," the stewardess said, finally managing to drag her eyes away from Blake's smiling profile. "Your wedding dress was beautiful. I just loved the color . . . sort of oyster pink, if there is such a shade."

"Thank you." Kate knew her smile was nowhere near

as friendly as Blake's had been. She wasn't an actress. She couldn't lie with every movement of her body and with every twist of her features.

Blake's charm vanished the moment the young woman turned her back. He quickly pulled his arm away from Kate's shoulders, then adjusted his seat to the reclining position and closed his eyes. He remained silent and unmoving until a second stewardess arrived with her trolley, ready to serve them a meal. In front of this new audience, Blake's affection returned as swiftly as if it had been flicked on by a switch. He played to perfection the part of the doting newlywed husband, but Kate cringed under the lash of his honeyed words. She flinched every time his hands touched her in a false caress. It would be easier to tolerate his anger, she thought, if he allowed it to show.

Kate saw Joni as soon as the plane door swung open, filling the aircraft with a rush of hot, moisture-laden air. Even at this distance, Kate could see that Joni looked tanned and cool in an ice-blue muslin dress that blew softly around her legs in the early morning breeze. She stood on a patch of grass at the edge of the tarmac, waving madly until Blake spotted her and waved back with equal enthusiasm.

He climbed swiftly down the rickety metal steps and strode across the strip of heat-softened runway. He scooped Joni into his arms, and Kate, following as slowly as she could, still couldn't avoid hearing their rapturous exchange of greetings.

A middle-aged man, short, thin and with a thatch of curly gray hair, stood to one side of Joni. Kate noticed the likeness between the two, although the man was far from handsome and Joni looked prettier than ever. His gaze was watchful and his expression unreadable as he watched the reunion scene being played out in front of him.

Joni finally wriggled free of Blake's embrace, pushing her short curls out of her eyes with a casual, graceful gesture. Kate started to feel more dowdy by the second. Her cotton dress stuck to her back, damp with sweat, and the skirt was crushed from sitting for so many hours in one position.

"Hello, Kate," Joni said with a polite smile. "Was it a rotten journey? You look completely wiped out."

"The flight was fine, but Blake and I didn't get much sleep the night before we left the States. It was our wedding night, you know." Kate flashed a smile that was every bit as polite as Joni's. She felt Blake move at her side, but ignored him. Three of them could play at this game, she thought grimly. She extended her hand toward the middle-aged man, who had remained silent. "You must be Sacha Stein," she said. "I've heard so much about you and your work. It's a great pleasure to meet you in person."

"Mrs. Harrington." Sacha Stein inclined his head, shaking Kate's hand between two of his own.

"Oh, but you must call me Kate," she said, wondering if anybody's facial muscles had ever been known to crack from insincere smiling.

"And please call me Sacha."

Joni, impatient with three minutes of conversation that had totally excluded her, grabbed hold of Blake's arm and twisted herself around him exactly as she had done at Windhaven. "The car's over there outside the Customs Hall," she said, nodding vaguely. She couldn't point, because her hands were fully occupied in clinging to Blake. "You don't mind if Blake and I keep each other company, do you, Kate? We have so much to talk about. The movie...the scenes we'll be shooting tomorrow...things you don't know anything about."

"Of course I don't mind," Kate said. "Blake and I have the rest of our lives to spend together. We're married."

Joni didn't seem to appreciate this reminder of the legal realities of the situation. She wound herself a fraction more tightly around Blake's arm—any tighter and she'll cut off his circulation, Kate thought—and then led the way into the Customs and Immigration Hall. Sacha raised his arm in a seemingly vague signal, and immediately two young

Fijians appeared, materializing, as far as Kate could see, from behind a clump of palm trees.

"LeRoy, Ed. Take care of Mr. Harrington's luggage." Almost as an afterthought, he added, "This is Mrs. Harrington."

LeRoy and Ed shook hands, enquired after her journey, and then disappeared as quickly as they had arrived.

"They work for me," Sacha Stein said, as vague as before, except that Kate was sure Sacha was never vague about anything that had the least importance to his work.

In other circumstances, she would have enjoyed hearing the soft lilt of the Islanders' English as she and Blake passed through the Customs and Immigration section of the airport. There was no air conditioning in the building, and the huge ceiling fans stirred the air—and the flies—with a lethargy reminiscent of a 1930 movie. Even though she felt so lonely, Kate spared a moment to admire the proud bearing of the island policemen, who wore a dashing uniform of a white, calf-length skirt and a dark, military-style jacket. The strange combination, far from looking ridiculous, appeared unexpectedly smart. From the number of souvenir police dolls she could see dotted around the airport stores, the Fijians were well aware of the tourist appeal of their law enforcement officers.

She endured the chauffeur-driven journey from the airport to the hotel by keeping her mind as blank as possible. She forced herself to admire the scenery flashing past the car windows, and she ignored the unceasing, intimate conversation between Joni and her husband. Her husband! she thought, then blanked her mind again before the irony of her situation could cause another sharp stab of pain somewhere in the region of her stomach.

Sacha glanced at his daughter from time to time, but made no effort to curb her monopoly of Blake's attention. Nor did he make much effort to describe to Kate where she was going. He informed her that the airport was situated on Viti Levu, the largest of the chain of Fijian Islands, and that they were driving to a resort hotel on the tropical side of the island. The prevailing trade winds, he explained briefly, gave one side of the islands a typically lush tropical climate, while the other side remained dry and semi-barren. "It's the windward side that has the rain," he said. "Or is it the leeward?" He dismissed any further consideration of the problem. "God-awful hour in the morning your plane arrived from the States," he said to Kate.

As far as he was concerned, this was the end of his efforts to introduce her to the beauties of Fiji. He closed his eyes and leaned back in his corner seat.

She seemed to be sending a lot of people to sleep recently, Kate thought, then made herself feel angry so that she wouldn't give way to self-pity. Whatever Blake thought she had done, she was his wife, and there was no justification for allowing two artistic egomaniacs to treat her so rudely. She twisted in her seat, about to force Blake to answer some question—she didn't know what, anything so that he would take his attention away from Joni—but her question faded away unspoken as she saw Blake touch Sacha's arm.

"What about the helicopter scene?" Blake asked. "Has it been re-taken, Sacha?" His voice seemed casual, almost too casual, but his hands betrayed him. His fists were clenched tight, the knuckles gleaming white as he strained to keep his features expressionless. Suddenly aware of Kate's glaze fixed on his hands, he thrust them out of sight at his sides.

There was no immediate answer from Sacha, and the tension in the car rose. Even Joni had nothing to say. "You're not asleep, dammit," Blake said. "Answer me, Sacha. Has that scene been re-taken?"

Sacha opened his eyes. "It was successfully reshot the day you left the island."

"I see you didn't waste any time in unnecessary mourning," Blake said tersely.

"This movie is already half a million over budget," Sacha snapped. "What the hell did you expect me to do? Keep the helicopter crew on the payroll for an extra month or so while you came to terms with yourself?"

"I've worked with you for six years, Sacha. I didn't expect anything." Blake turned and glanced out of the window. "We're nearly at the hotel," he said. "What time do you want me on the set tomorrow? When do you start shooting?"

"At daybreak. There's a call sheet and a shooting script waiting in your suite, Blake, which you should study tonight. We took every scene that didn't have you in it while you were away. Now we're going to need you on the set from dawn to dusk. We have to get these location shots wrapped up. We're not only half a million over budget, we're also three months behind schedule. The investment bankers in New York are beginning to sound like a Greek chorus of doom."

"I'll be ready to start shooting first thing tomorrow morning," Blake said quietly.

Sacha appeared relieved that Blake's response had been so moderate. He allowed himself to look marginally more cheerful, and even managed to smile pleasantly at Kate when the chauffeur parked the car in front of an impressively modern resort hotel.

"I'll send somebody around tomorrow to entertain you, Mrs. Harrington . . . er . . . Kate. I expect you'll want to see the island, right?"

"Right," Kate replied. It was clear she was not going to be welcome on the set, and Joni shot her a glance of mingled spite and triumph.

"It's tough being the wife of a movie star. Are you finding that out, Kate?"

She wished she could think of something terribly clever or cutting to say. All she could think of was the truth. "I'm tired," she said. "Blake, could we please go to our room?"

Perhaps she looked exhausted enough to convince Sacha that, if he wasn't careful, he might find his superstar with a sick wife on his hands. For whatever reasons, he was suddenly all solicitude, whisking Blake and Kate away to their suite with a speed and efficiency that banished all his previous vagueness. When Joni suggested she might stay and go over tomorrow's script with Blake, Sacha hustled her out of the room without even bothering to comment on her suggestion.

Kate and Blake were left standing together in the middle of their private sitting room. Neither of them could find anything to say.

"It's a nice hotel," Kate said at last.

"Yes, it is." Blake opened one of his suitcases and began rummaging carelessly through its contents. "I'm going swimming in the lagoon." His curt tone indicated he was not looking for company.

"Fine," she said, not daring to suggest she should join him. "I guess I'll take a shower. I feel tired, and perhaps some cold water will revive me."

"Your face is too pale," he said brusquely, looking straight at her for the first time in hours. "Maybe you should take a nap or something."

There was a moment of tense silence in the room, then he pulled his swimsuit from the suitcase and slammed down the lid with unnecessary violence. "See you around," he said and went out of the room.

Kate had no energy for unpacking. She shook out a few dresses and placed them on hangers in one of the wall closets. She piled a few pairs of shoes in a corner of the bedroom, and put a stack of lacy underwear in one of the dresser drawers. Not bothering to do anything more, she went into the bathroom and stepped into the shower, turning it on full force. She let the water cascade over her in a burning stream for a long time while she shampooed her long hair. Slowly, she adjusted the faucets until the biting needles of spray became as cold as she could tolerate. Gradually her aching body began to feel human once again.

She hadn't brought any clean clothes into the bathroom with her, so she draped a towel loosely around her body and wandered back into the bedroom. Perhaps, having taken a cold shower, she would be capable of thinking more constructively.

She heard the scratch of a key in the lock, and turned around just as Blake entered the room. He had presumably showered and shaved at some beachside facility, for his dark stubble of beard was gone, and he had changed into cutoff jeans and a clean cotton shirt. He looked so much like the Blake Koehler she had fallen in love with that Kate felt her heart contract in a fierce, involuntary surge of longing. It was crazy. They were behaving like a couple of feuding teen-agers. They couldn't throw their marriage away because of a single misunderstanding.

"Blake..." Fatigue and suppressed emotion made her speak his name with a husky sensuality.

He acknowledged her presence with a nod, tossing his bundle of damp clothing on a nearby chair. "What do you want?" For a moment his gaze skimmed over her, then abruptly he turned away. "What is it?" he repeated, sitting in a chair by the window and starting to flick through the pages of his call sheet.

She knelt down beside his chair, reaching up to still the restless movement of his hands. "Blake, don't turn away from me. Surely you don't want our marriage to continue this way. Whatever you think of me, wouldn't it be better if we tried to be friends? Can't we start again, Blake, *please?*" Her words died away in a hopeless whisper as he turned around to face her, his eyes bright with scorn.

"Tighten your bath towel, honey. You're displaying too much cleavage." He watched tauntingly while she secured the towel with fingers that trembled slightly. "Next time you set out to seduce me, remember I've been working around movie sets for over ten years. I've seen more naked women than most men can even fantasize about, and, believe me, after the first thousand or so, you all look the same."

She pulled herself away from him, more hurt than if he

had physically abused her. "Why do you constantly try to humiliate me?" she asked. "At Windhaven you wanted to make love to me. You told me you ... cared for me. Why has it all changed now?"

His face tightened. "What difference does it make to you? You've got your new checkbook, and my bank balance should make your eyes gleam. Run on out to the local stores and entertain yourself. I believe there's an expensive jewelers right in the hotel lobby. Don't waste your time hoping you can change my opinion of you, because you can't."

"What makes you think I'll stay here if you keep insulting me the way you are at the moment?"

"The day you walk away from me is the day I cancel your bank credit, honey. I think I can count on having you around for as long as I'm prepared to keep you."

"You're despicable, Blake," she said in a voice harsh with pain.

He laughed. "Isn't this marriage working out quite the way you planned it, sugar baby? Did you imagine you'd have me wrapped around your elegant little fingers by the time I discovered the truth about your Daddy's unfortunate financial situation? Or perhaps you hoped I'd be so addicted to your performance in our bed that I wouldn't care about the stratagems you used to get me there?" Cruelly, he allowed his gaze to roam in an insulting inventory of her body. "You're stacked, honey, but not quite that spectacular."

There was no way to hide herself from the deliberate cruelty of his words. He wanted to insult her. He wanted to drive her away. "I'm sorry, Blake," she said tonelessly. "Whatever you believe, I didn't deceive you."

"No," he agreed bleakly. "You didn't deceive me. I deceived myself." He pulled the pages of the shooting script toward him and bent down to scan the first page. He gave no indication that he was aware Kate was still in the room. His forehead wrinkled in concentration, and his lips moved silently as he began to memorize the words in front of him.

"I'll get dressed," Kate said. There seemed nothing else to say. "In case you want to know where I am, I'll find the swimming pool and take a nap in a lounge chair."

"Don't bother to rush back. I'll be working all day, and Joni and I have a date for dinner tonight." He didn't look up from the printed page, but he must have heard her sudden intake of breath. "Have fun," he added mockingly.

"I will! I'll make sure of that!" Misery gave a sharp point to her words, and for a moment it looked as if Blake might say something further. The moment passed and, with an indifferent shrug of his shoulders, he returned to studying the script. Kate slammed the door of their room with a force that vibrated along the length of the corridor. The noise did nothing whatsoever to soothe the gnawing pain that squeezed at her heart.

- 10 -

SACHA DID NOT keep his promise to provide Kate with a tour guide the next day. She had traveled overseas many times before and should have been capable of organizing tours for herself, but she was gripped by the devastating lethargy of depression. She recognized the familiar symptoms of loneliness, but here in Fiji her usual cure was not available to her. In Wisconsin, her excess love and energy had all been channeled into caring for the children at the Center. Here she had nothing to do but lie in the sun—the everlasting, unchanging sun—and think about Blake. She spent her days swimming up and down the hotel pool, or walking along the sandy edges of the lagoon. Alone, always alone.

Blake was working eighteen-hour days. He left their rooms each morning before dawn and returned late at night with harsh lines of fatigue on his face. Sometimes Kate pretended to be asleep when he returned, and sometimes she didn't bother. It made no difference. He rarely spoke to her, and when he did it was only to make a remark necessary for the organization of their daily lives. There were two beds in the suite; otherwise, Kate would have insisted on taking a separate room. She could not have born lying in bed at night, wondering at each moment when their bodies might accidentally touch.

Sunday was no different from the days that had preceded it. Blake left their suite before dawn. "I'll be back late," he said. He said the same thing every morning.

"You're working today? But it's Sunday!"

"The technical crews are on triple pay, so they don't care. And Joni and I are anxious to get this movie wrapped up as soon as we can."

"Aren't you enjoying yourselves?" she flashed. "Haven't you reached the love scenes yet?"

There was a tiny pause before he replied. "I don't need to wait for a scene in a movie to make love to Joni," he said.

Kate stared dry-eyed at the door as he slammed it shut behind him. She laughed, then clamped her lips together as she recognized the thin note of approaching hysteria. She flung back the covers with a gesture of revulsion. Today, whatever Blake thought of her decision, she was going to visit the movie set. If he was in love with Joni, it would be better to face up to the truth.

It was embarrassing to have to ask the hotel staff where her husband was working, but the receptionist she spoke to was friendly and helpful, and found a cheerful cab driver to take Kate over the bumpy roads to where the movie was being shot. The set was built in a breathtakingly lovely bay, sheltered by palm trees. A low-lying white villa was just visible through a screen of tropical foliage.

A guard stopped the cab some distance from the beach. "I'm Mrs. Harrington," Kate said as she searched in her purse for money to pay off the driver. The guard saluted and gave her a wide grin as he let her through the barricade.

She moved as inconspicuously as she could to a corner where she could observe the activity. Sacha was talking intently to Blake, Joni, and another actor, who moved through a series of actions while camera, lighting, and sound technicians followed them around. Blake kept walking backwards and forwards between a clump of bushes and the middle of the beach. The camera crew seemed to be having difficulty following him.

Eventually Sacha and the cameramen were satisfied. Blake disappeared into the bush, and the other actor gripped Joni loosely by the waist. As soon as Sacha seated himself in a canvas chair, total silence fell. Sacha raised his hand, and Joni burst into action. The man holding her was trying to force her into a boat, and she was struggling to get free. She wrenched herself out of the man's grip with a vicious kick to his groin. The kick was so realistic that Kate actually winced.

Joni ran up the beach, screaming on a high-pitched note of panic that left Kate's palms wet with tension. Her attacker pounded over the sand behind her, and Joni called a man's name in a last, desperate bid for help. Blake exploded out of concealment, running at breakneck speed along the precise lines traced out by the cameramen.

Although Kate knew nothing of the movie's plot, she had no difficulty recognizing Blake's portrayal of agonizing indecision as his gaze flashed over the scene in front of him. Looking intently at his face, Kate could tell the precise moment when he decided to raise his gun and fire at Joni's attacker. The wounded man gave the impression of being flung into the air by the force of Blake's shot, and blood gushed from his stomach, soaking into the sand. For several terrible seconds, Kate wondered if she had actually seen a fatal accident.

"Okay. Cut!" Sacha stood up from his chair and the young actor sprang to his feet, brushing sand from his jeans and holding the blood-spattered shirt away from his body. "Any problems?" Sacha asked the crews in general.

He received quick, negative responses from the various technicians. "I kept the blood off the jeans," said the actor. "The plastic bag worked fine. But I'll need a clean shirt."

"Fifteen minutes for wardrobe and makeup to set it up again. Then we'll shoot it."

Kate realized she hadn't even witnessed a moment of filming, let alone a violent accident. The scene she had found so brutally convincing had merely been a rehearsal! She was so engrossed in the activities on the set that she forgot all about remaining inconspicuously to one side and started to walk to a better position. She jumped when a pleasant voice spoke behind her.

"Hello, I'm Peter Drake. Could you possibly be the mysterious Mrs. Blake Harrington? Or are there two females, newly arrived in Fiji, who look so tantalizing from the rear?"

She turned round, smiling as she held out her hand. "I am Kate Harrington, but I'm not sure that I qualify as being mysterious. I'm not even wearing sunglasses!"

Peter Drake shook her hand with a flourish. "On the contrary, Mrs. Harrington, you're mysterious *and* beautiful. Every man on the set has been dying to meet you. We knew any woman who captured Blake's wandering eye would have to be special, but even we didn't guess just how special."

"That's a very smooth line, Mr. Drake, and you delivered it beautifully. You must be an actor."

She saw his face fall, and knew she had blundered. "I'm sorry," she added quickly. "There are probably less than a dozen women in America who wouldn't recognize you, and I happen to be one of them. I haven't gone to the movies for the last few years."

Peter Drake's blue eyes lit up with a rueful grin. "Well, I knew I hadn't reached your husband's superstar status yet, and I didn't expect a full-scale swoon when you heard my name. But I did at least expect a flicker of recognition!"

"I'll tell you something," she said a little breathlessly, warming to his friendly manner. "I didn't even recognize Blake when we first met. Does that make you feel a bit better?"

"It leaves me feeling intrigued," Peter replied. Before he could say more, Sacha signaled for silence. The callboy banged the clapperboard, and the scene once again began to unroll in front of them. Joni was good, Kate had to admit reluctantly. She played her part with a gritty determination that had absolutely nothing in common with the affected, self-centered young woman Kate had seen off the set.

"Joni is a good actress," she said to Peter with just the hint of a question in her voice.

"Anybody who works with Sacha, even if she's his daughter, has to be the best," Peter said simply. "He's a total perfectionist. He's hell to work with. He doesn't know the meaning of honesty while he's making a movie. He'll lie, beg, steal, corrupt—anything, as long as the movie gets produced *his* way. And in spite of that, most actors would willingly sell their souls to get to work with him. He's brilliant."

Kate watched the rest of the morning's shooting and concluded Peter was correct. All the actors were good, although Joni and Blake seemed to have that special tautness and control that separated the truly great actor from the merely very good.

The last take of the morning was a complex fight scene requiring several fast and precisely-timed moves, if the actors were to avoid hurting each other while still giving a convincing impression of sustained violence. Kate found it tiring simply to watch the many rehearsals. For the actors, under the blazing noon sun, it must have been totally exhausting. Blake seemed to be constantly in the middle of a great many flying fists and gleaming knife blades. She felt sick with fright at the thought of him lying injured, and she hated the way her shivering body betrayed her mental weakness. Why should she care so much about a man who constantly humiliated her? When the shooting finally started, she was careful to keep her face expressionless, but she could do nothing about the tumultuous state of her inner feelings.

The scene had been rehearsed so many times that she recognized the error at once when one of the stuntmen missed his footing and fell into the path of another actor. She saw instantly that his fall would leave the outstretched steel of a switchblade pointed straight at Blake's heart. She gave an involuntary cry of dismay as she watched her husband hurtle inevitably toward the blade.

Blake heard her voice and looked up, startled. He visibly lost his concentration when he saw Kate, and tripped over the fallen stuntman, causing the knife to plunge sickeningly deep into his thigh.

"Cut!" Sacha yelled. "What the hell is going on there? Can't any of you clowns stand on your feet for five minutes?"

Blake got up, wiping grains of sand from his mouth with the back of his hand. There wasn't a trace of blood to be seen. A makeup man rushed over to him, but Blake pushed him impatiently aside and strode over to Kate. "What are you doing here?" he asked tautly.

"I wanted to see you working." Her cheeks flamed with embarrassment at the curtness of his tone. "Are you . . . Are you hurt?"

"Of course not."

"But the knife—"

"For God's sake, Kate, they all have retracting plastic blades. They couldn't hurt a newborn baby."

"Oh . . . I'm sorry. I didn't know."

Blake said nothing more and Kate, only too aware of Peter Drake's presence, fell silent as well. Sacha signaled the retaking of the scene, and Blake went quickly back to the set.

There were four more takes before the scene was successfully wrapped up. On each of the three failures, Kate knew the fault had been Blake's. His concentration seemed to have vanished, and he was guilty of three slight mistimings that threw off the other actors, ruining the scene.

"Lunch!" Sacha called abruptly when the shooting was finally over. He walked directly across to Kate, although he had given no previous indication of having noticed her arrival. Joni walked simultaneously onto the set and began to talk softly to Blake.

"Mrs. Harrington," Sacha said, nodding his head in greeting. He paused, searching his memory. "That is . . . er . . . Kate. Nice to see you."

"It's good to be here," she replied coolly. Out of the corner of her eye, she tried to watch Blake and Joni.

With no further attempt at courtesy, Sacha said bluntly, "Please don't come to the set again, Kate. You distract Blake, and he's already under too much pressure to be able to cope with any more."

"I don't understand," Kate said, although she was afraid she understood only too well.

Sacha didn't bother to explain his order. He turned to Peter Drake, who was still hovering close by, not quite out of earshot. "I won't need you this afternoon; the schedule's already shot to hell. Why don't you take Kate out to lunch? Perhaps you could show her some of the local beauty spots." There was no doubt that his words were a command, not a request.

"It would be my pleasure," Peter said easily. "Come on, Kate, let me take you away from this madhouse before everybody finds out I've been awarded the prize."

She was grateful to him for smoothing over the awkwardness of Sacha's brusque dismissal, and even more grateful when he drove her to a pleasant local restaurant, pointing out places of interest on the way. He asked her casually how she had met Blake, and refrained from pressing her to expand on her vague replies. Once they had ordered lunch, he chatted genially about Viti Levu and the other Fijian islands he had visited. There were still a few places in the region, he said, where the natives were hostile to intruders, and there were plenty of smaller islands that had never been fully mapped. Some of the uncharted islands were large enough to be inhabited.

"When we can switch on our television sets and see close-up shots of the planet Saturn, it's hard to believe there are places in our own world that are still a mystery," Kate said.

"Yes," Peter agreed. "There's a lot of ocean out there waiting to reveal its secrets." He fell silent while the waiter poured them each a cup of coffee, then he said gently, "Do you want to talk about anything special, Kate? The movie... What it's like to work for Sacha..."

She knew he was curious about her relationship with Blake, but she also sensed genuine kindness behind his questions.

"Tell me the story of the movie," she said.

"It's a good plot. Blake is playing the part of an undercover agent for one of the federal agencies. He's sent to infiltrate a major arms-smuggling ring that's suspected of shipping military supplies to Africa and the Middle East. Joni is playing a promiscuous teen-age criminal, supposedly the girl friend of the master criminal."

"Who's the master criminal?" Kate asked.

"I am. Do you think I look the type?"

"No." She laughed. "I imagined somebody bald and fat, smoking an evil-smelling cigar."

"Sacha doesn't go much for stereotypes. My character represents the new breed of criminal. I'm supposed to be well educated and, therefore, twice as hard to catch. In the movie, I personally organize my arms shipments on the latest model computer."

"It sounds like an adventure movie!"

"No, it's not really. The character Blake is playing falls in love with Joni, and the movie's main interest depends on Blake's ability to portray a man torn between loyalty to the law and love for a woman who is outside society's normal moral code. Sacha was right when he said Blake is under a lot of pressure right now. The success of the movie rides on his acting ability."

"But he's already a superstar! Surely everybody agrees he can act."

For the first time Peter's smile was tinged with cynicism. "My dear Kate, even you can't be naïve enough to think that every movie star can act! Blake made his name in two space adventures. He spent most of his time in those two movies striding around in a silver cape and showing off his incredibly sexy body. In this movie he has to *act,* and that's altogether a different story."

"You mean . . . he isn't succeeding?"

"I mean he's brilliant. But underneath the cool exterior Blake presents to the world, there lies a man who's as insecure as all the rest of us actors. He'll never be convinced he's a decent actor until he's ready to retire from movie-making." There was a short pause while Peter looked out of the window at the harbor, taking care to avoid Kate's eyes. "Being married to Blake will never be easy," he said.

She didn't pretend not to understand him. "Is there anything else you think I should know, Peter? You may as well tell me it all."

"Do you know about Kevin?" he asked slowly. "Do you know why Blake left Fiji so suddenly?"

"No," she said, her throat dry. "Tell me about it."

"Well, you must know that Blake originally started in the movie business as a stuntman. Kevin was his partner and a great guy, probably Blake's closest personal friend. They'd been at sea together, I believe. Maybe you knew him?"

Kate shook her head.

"Kevin was in charge of the stunts for this movie, which happens to end in a gun battle between the arms smugglers and a slew of law enforcement agents. At one point, a helicopter was supposed to fly over and whisk Blake out of a moving car so that he could escape from the gang.

Kevin was the man let down from the helicopter to pull Blake off the roof of the getaway car. Normally the whole rescue would have been performed by stand ins, but Blake insisted on doing it himself. The closeup shots are more convincing, naturally, if they aren't faked-in afterwards."

"It sounds . . . very dangerous."

"It's not the most dangerous stunt ever devised, but it requires split-second timing and muscles of steel on the part of the man being pulled from the roof of the car *and* the man who's supporting him on a cable wire let down from the helicopter."

"What happened?"

"There was a freak failure of the equipment. The cable supporting Kevin snapped, his backup cable buckled under the strain, and Kevin was dragged under the wheels of Blake's car. He died of a broken back and a ruptured spleen."

Kate turned white as she visualized the scene conjured up by Peter's all-too-vivid description. "It wasn't Blake's fault," Peter said. "It was nobody's fault, in fact. At least three different people, including Kevin, checked every inch of those cables. Blake blamed himself, though, because he said a working stuntman in tiptop condition would have been able to hold Kevin on top of the car."

"Is that true?" Kate asked.

"No. The helicopter was moving in one direction and the car in another. As it was, Blake dislocated his shoulder and badly damaged his hip by throwing himself off the car in an effort to grab hold of Kevin. He was hospitalized for a week, and refused to see any of us. When Sacha went to pick him up at the local hospital, he'd checked himself out and disappeared. He just vanished. You probably know better than the rest of us where he went and what he did?" Peter's voice rose in an unmistakable question.

"Yes," Kate said. "I know where he went. He went home to Windhaven."

"Windhaven?"

"His parents' farm."

"Oh, I see. Joni did say she finally ran him to earth in Wisconsin. Sacha was more cut up about Kevin's death than he cared to admit, and, when Blake disappeared, he just about went berserk. We've had a tough few weeks out here, I can tell you, while you and Blake were getting yourselves married."

"I'm sorry," Kate said inadequately.

"You've brought him back to the movie, and that's what counts. For a while there, we all wondered if he would refuse to continue."

Kate stood up abruptly. "I'm grateful to you, Peter, for everything you've told me. Could you drive me back to the hotel now?"

"Sure. And in return, you can tell me about yourself. What did you do before you married Blake Harrington? Apart from being the most beautiful girl in Wisconsin?"

She gave him a brief account of her past history during their drive back to her hotel. She glossed over the details of her marriage to Steven and curbed her enthusiasm when describing her work as a teacher at the Center for Autistic Children. Peter listened to her intently, and left her at her hotel with repeated comments on how much he had enjoyed their afternoon together.

"Next time we're both free, let me show you some spots of interest on Viti Levu. There are a couple of special places I'd enjoy taking you to."

"I'd like that." Kate's smile was full of genuine warmth. Peter was not only friendly, he was also a thoughtful and intelligent companion. She would enjoy exploring the island with him.

She parted from him feeling more at ease with herself than she had in days. She had become too egocentric, she decided, too concerned with her own pride. She had been wrong to assume that all the tensions in her marriage sprang from a single cause. She carried hurts from her previous relationships, so she ought to be able to understand that

Blake—an experienced, hard-living man of thirty-five—didn't come to her completely unscarred. It was up to her to convince him that she wasn't the scheming gold digger he assumed her to be, and she couldn't do that if she maintained a wall of proud, self-righteous silence.

She was secretly pleased when he arrived at the hotel early that evening, although she forced herself to hide her reaction. It was the first time he had returned before dark.

"I didn't expect to find you here," he said, squashing her moment of pleasure. "Aren't you having dinner with Peter Drake?"

"No." Kate pushed nervously at a loose strand of hair. Faced with the reality of Blake's hostility, her plans for a reconciliation seemed faintly ridiculous. "Are you eating dinner with . . . with somebody else tonight, Blake?"

"No."

"Could we . . . Couldn't we eat together?"

"I guess we can have dinner together, if you want." He didn't look at her as he answered. "I know a good Indian restaurant near here."

"I'll enjoy that," she said, keeping her response casual. "If you don't mind waiting, it will only take me a couple of minutes to get ready."

Blake summoned a cab to take them to the small Indian restaurant overlooking the sea. It was a quiet place, and most of the other diners were Indians, local residents of Viti Levu. Both Blake and Kate found conversation difficult at first, and they examined the handwritten menu with painful concentration. Gradually, some of the tension eased away under the pleasure of tasting exotic new dishes and experimenting with some sickly-sweet local fruit punch. She asked him some questions about the islands, and he told her about Captain Cook's journeys around the South Pacific and his incredible feat in accurately charting so many tiny dots of land in the vast stretches of Pacific Ocean. "He was an extraordinary man," Blake said. "He was the son of a farm laborer from northern England, and he made his way to the top by sheer dogged determination. Once he realized what skills were needed to become a great navigator, he simply sat down and taught them to himself: mathematics, trigonometry, astronomy. He was one of the first naval officers to test the theories about a link between sailors' diets and scurvy. Before his voyages to the South Seas, navy ships used to be built to accommodate twice the size of crew that was needed because the naval authorities knew that half the sailors would die of scurvy before the end of the journey. Captain Cook showed that if you kept the sailors' quarters disinfected, and if you fed them fresh fruit and vegetables, nobody needed to die of scurvy."

"Wasn't he killed here in these islands?" Kate asked. "I know the Fijians were originally very fierce warriors."

"No, he wasn't killed here. He died in Hawaii. The natives thought he was a god when his ship first anchored offshore. Later they decided he wasn't a god, and killed him to prove their point."

Kate shuddered. "It seems a brutal end for a man who was only interested in scientific discovery."

"The eighteenth century was a brutal age. Captain Cook had six children and not one of them survived to reach middle age. Three of his sons were killed at sea, and two of them died as infants before he ever saw them."

"I couldn't have stood it if I'd been his wife," she said. "Can you imagine what it must have been like, waiting at home for years at a stretch, hearing no news, wondering if your husband was alive or dead? And then to lose two of your children...Whatever Captain Cook may have endured, I think it was harder to be his wife."

"Perhaps you're right." Blake's gaze softened as he looked at Kate's flushed cheeks and sparkling eyes. "Mrs. Cook should have had you there to defend her rights. I'm sure you'd never have allowed her husband to go gallivanting off to the South Seas, leaving her behind to mind the house and watch over the babies!"

"Well, I do think women in those days had a pretty rough time of it."

"I can see the light of battle starting to gleam in your eyes, Kate. Any minute now you'll be telling me that, if the founding fathers had only written equal rights for women into the Constitution, the world would be a better place."

She couldn't help smiling. "I don't fight lost causes," she said. "I save my feminist arguments for people who can be converted. And since the founding fathers have been dead for about two hundred years, I don't see much point in trying to rewrite history."

"Very wise of you," he murmured. "I can see I married a clever wom . . ." His words died away. "Have you finished your coffee?" he asked curtly, pushing his chair away from the table. "I need to get back to the hotel since I have an early start tomorrow morning."

"Yes, I've finished." She knew the fragile harmony of their mood was shattered and would not easily be recalled.

Blake hailed another cab and they drove back to the hotel in tense silence, seated as far away from each other as the rear seat of the cab would permit.

He still avoided talking to her even when they were in their hotel suite again. Kate undressed in the bathroom, and emerged in her nightgown to find him pacing restlessly around the bedroom. His eyes ran over her in a quick, involuntary appraisal, and she saw a muscle flicker in the tightly-clenched line of his jaw.

"I'm going out for a walk," he said.

"Please don't go." Her softly-spoken plea halted him at the door of the suite. "Blake . . . couldn't we . . . talk a little?"

"What about?"

"Our marriage. Please, Blake." She forced down all her useless thoughts of pride and dignity and ran across the room to catch hold of his arm.

His whole body became utterly still except for a single pulse beating rapidly at the base of his throat. Tentatively, she rested her hand against his chest. She could feel his heart racing beneath her outspread fingers.

His free hand caught her fingers, pushing them roughly away. "We have no marriage to discuss," he said. His voice was expressionless, and his hand remained on the door handle, as if at any moment he would go out: But his knuckles gleamed white, betraying the rigid control he was having to exert over his emotions.

"But we *are* married, Blake. Do you plan to go on denying the truth of that fact forever?"

"I've told you we have no real marriage," he said harshly. "We have a business arrangement."

"You don't mean that, Blake," she said softly. "I know you want to make love to me."

"You know nothing, damn you!" His rigid control snapped, and he jerked her against his body without any trace of tenderness. His mouth was hot and aggressive as he dragged her head around to cover her lips in a hard kiss.

"Do you want sex included in our business arrangement, Kate, is that it?" He kissed her again, parting her lips with a brutality that contained no trace of love. "Is that what you want, Kate?" he repeated cruelly when he finally thrust her away.

"Is it what *you* want? Cold sex instead of warm love?"

"Yes, damn you, that's what I want! I know you're a mercenary conniver so why should I keep remembering... Why should I torment myself with false memories of the way you seemed to be at Windhaven?"

She sensed the hunger behind his words and felt herself respond to the raw need that blazed in his eyes for a few, unguarded seconds. She moved back into his arms, arching against his body and giving a little moan of pleasure as he pushed aside the thin straps of her nightgown and caressed the smooth skin of her back.

"You're so beautiful," he said as he kissed her. "Oh, God! Why did you have to be so beautiful?"

"Make love to me, Blake," she whispered.

"No!" The denial seemed to be torn from him, and he

pushed her away with hands that shook. "No!" he said again. "I'm going for a walk."

"Am I such a threat?" she asked softly.

"Yes," he breathed. "When I'm with you, you're a fever in my blood. At least if I'm away from you, I can remember what sort of woman you really are."

"You don't know what I really am, Blake," she said sadly.

"I'm leaving Viti Levu before dawn tomorrow morning," he said at last. "A few of us will be shooting scenes on another island for a couple of days. When I come back, perhaps we can talk."

"We could talk now, Blake. You just don't want to listen."

He shrugged. "I'm going for a walk, Kate. Don't bother to wait up."

- 11 -

Kate was glad to receive a telephone call from Peter Drake the next morning. She had assumed he would be leaving Viti Levu with Blake and the rest of the crew, and she was pleased to find she was mistaken.

"Most of my location shots have been filmed," Peter said. "I've got nothing to do for the next two days. How about coming on a tour of the island with me, Kate?"

"I'd enjoy that," she said sincerely.

He took her first to Suva, Fiji's capital city, a bustling, picturesque port town. The main streets were lined with pepper trees, and the parks and gardens blossomed with a riot of bright tropical flowers. The markets, designed to appeal to tourists, were crowded with stalls selling wood carvings, cheap silver jewelry, and souvenir dolls. Many of the stalls were owned by Indians, and the gold-threaded saris of the women gleamed in the sunlight, adding to the impression of tropical exuberance.

After visiting Government House, Peter took her to the town of Lautoka, where they embarked on a motor launch. The cruiser took them on an unforgettable tour of the sixty-mile chain of Yasawa Islands, still populated entirely by native Fijians, living much as they had done for the five centuries prior to the arrival of Western traders and missionaries. There were no East Indians on any of these islands, and the tour guide told Kate that the Indians on Viti Levu had been imported as virtual slave labor in the nineteenth century in order to work the sugarcane fields. Their unceasing hard work, which contrasted strongly with the more easygoing attitude of the native Fijians, had resulted in most of the commerce of the country falling into their hands. The native Fijians, however, still owned all the land. Foreigners could only rent property, not buy it.

Peter left Kate at the door of her hotel room late at night. She felt pleasantly tired and relaxed, intensely grateful to Peter because, for a short while, he had helped her to push the problems of her marriage to the background of her mind.

"May I pick you up at the same time tomorrow?" he asked. "There's somewhere special I want to show you."

"Sounds exciting."

"Not exciting," he said, "but I know you'll be interested."

Something in his voice warned her that tomorrow they would not be touring more of the major attractions. "What is it, Peter? Is something wrong?"

"Nothing at all," he assured her. He bent his head and brushed her cheek lightly with his mouth. "Thanks for being a fantastic companion," he said.

"I should be saying that to you," she replied as she slipped quickly into her room. Peter was a wonderful friend, and she didn't want anything to happen to alter that.

He picked her up after breakfast the next morning. "I'm taking you to a special school on the other side of the bay," he said. "When you told me about your work at the Center in Milwaukee, I knew you'd be interested. This is a residential facility that's only recently been opened. The staff is small and there's no resident doctor, but it's doing fabulous work."

"I certainly am interested," she said. "How did you find out about it, Peter? It's not the sort of research work I associate with handsome young movie stars."

He was silent for a long time. "I have a sister with multiple sclerosis," he said at last. "When somebody in your family is seriously ill, you develop a whole different perspective on things. I've been doing volunteer work at schools for handicapped children for quite a while."

"Oh, Peter, I'm so sorry about your sister!" Instinctively, Kate rested her hand on his arm in a gesture of comfort. "Is she much younger than you?"

"She's twelve," Peter said. "My parents had three sons, and they were ecstatic when Cindy arrived." For a few minutes his face was shadowed with pain. "The worst part of it is that they're always hoping for a cure. They read about miracle drugs being discovered for so many diseases, and they wake up each morning hoping that maybe today is going to be the day when Cindy's miracle will happen."

Kate's hand tightened against his arm, but she said nothing. What was there to say? One of the best things about her work at the Center had been the fact that autism was not life-threatening. Her daily work was filled with hope, because each small step toward self-sufficiency meant a greater chance of a useful life for the children she was teaching.

With an obvious effort, Peter shook off his depression. "We're nearly there," he said. "You'll like the school. It's designed for children with permanent physical handicaps who are capable of benefiting from special training. It's the only school on the island, so of course there's always a waiting list."

The director, a thin, elderly man, greeted them warmly.

Peter pulled out a huge box of candy from the back seat of the car and looked pleadingly at the director, who laughed good-naturedly. "I suppose I'll have to allow you to pass it out. But I keep telling you, Peter, there are only a dozen dentists in the whole of Fiji. The way you're handing out candy, soon all twelve of them will be kept busy taking care of the children in this school!"

"Next time I'll bring apples."

"That's what you promise every time."

"This is a friend of mine, Kate Harrington," Peter said, hastily changing the subject. "She was trained as a special education teacher back home in the States. Kate, this is Thomas Bligh, the director of the school."

Mr. Bligh insisted on conducting Kate on a personal tour of the school. By American standards, the facilities were sparse, with no expensive diagnostic machines and a minimum of therapeutic equipment. "Most of our children have very obvious physical problems," Mr. Bligh commented. "They're blind, or deaf, or paralyzed as the result of some accident. We have so few doctors and nurses in Fiji, and so few specially-trained teachers, that we can't afford to take in children with obscure medical problems. Our aim is to make the pupils as close to self-sufficient as we can, so that they can find employment once they leave here." Mr. Bligh's smile was tinged with sadness. "Our students learn very quickly that they can lead useful, productive lives in spite of their apparent handicaps. Our biggest problem is convincing other people of that fact."

"We certainly share that problem in the States," Kate said. "I guess it's always difficult for a healthy person to accept that a person's handicap is only that: a handicap, and not a sign that the person is incapable of doing anything useful."

Peter and Kate spent the afternoon playing with the children and watching their various forms of therapy. The school had a small garden leading down to a shallow lagoon, and all the children spent at least an hour a day splashing in the warm, salty water. The children regarded their time in the sea as enjoyable play, but Kate was impressed with the dedication of the three instructors, who managed to transform play into a learning experience that strengthened the children's muscles and increased their confidence in their own capabilities. Most of all, she was impressed by the way all three teachers were able to help all the children. Accustomed to the narrow specialization of therapists in the States, she found it enlightening to watch women who could teach Braille to one group of students and sign language to another. The third teacher, working with a group of children in wheelchairs, admitted that her formal training had been in Australia as a physiotherapist. She had "sort of picked up" basic teaching skills when she found out how badly they were needed.

They had so much to talk about on the way home that Kate scarcely noticed the gathering darkness, or realized how long she and Peter had been out together. She was enthusiastic about the open, informal atmosphere of the school and thanked Peter for taking her to see it. With a momentary flash of selfishness, she acknowledged to herself that nothing else could so effectively have kept her thoughts away from Blake for another whole day.

They stopped for a quick meal during the drive home, still talking about the school and its pupils, and then continued on. Kate was describing some of her own success stories to Peter when he drew the car to a halt outside her hotel. It seemed entirely natural to invite him into her suite while she looked for some photographs of one of her "star" pupils. Joey had entered the Milwaukee Center at the age of three, a frightened baby who screamed for hours at a stretch and seemed totally unaware of the world around him. He had left it four months ago, an almost normal eight year old, capable of entering second grade at his neighborhood school.

Kate pulled the photos out of a plastic folder, and Peter came to stand close by her, looking at the series of pictures which showed Joey's transformation from a thin, dirty toddler into a chubby eight year old. In the final photo his smile was so angelic that he looked as if he ought to be singing in the church choir.

"Why is he so dirty in these early pictures?" Peter asked. "Did his parents neglect him?"

"Not in the way you mean. But he became literally hysterical if anybody tried to put him in a bath or a shower, and eventually they gave up hope of keeping him clean. He was so thin because he would only eat cookies and drink one single brand of apple juice. If the local store happened to run out of that brand, he stopped drinking. He'd lived on cookies and juice for three straight months just before we finally took him into the Center."

They bent together over the pictures, studying the vivid record of Joey's transformation. When Kate finally turned round to put them away, she found herself trapped in Peter's arms.

He bent his head, intending to kiss her, and she tried to push him away. "Please don't, Peter," she said.

"Kate . . ." he said, then stopped as if uncertain how to continue. "I didn't mean that to happen, Kate." Neither of them heard the door open.

"Very charming," Blake said sarcastically. "I do apologize for interrupting."

Kate jerked out of Peter's arms, the pictures fluttering to the floor. Peter turned more slowly, meeting Blake's angry stare head-on.

"I was enjoying Kate's company," he said deliberately. "But I guess we can continue our conversation another day."

"Like hell you can!"

Peter ignored Blake's muttered comment and bent down to gather up the scattered photos. "Here, Kate. Thanks for a wonderful day."

He thrust the pictures into her hand, and she accepted them automatically. "Thank you for taking me with you," she said. She watched him leave the room, her eyes fixed intently on his retreating back. That way, she didn't have to look too closely at Blake.

The door closed with a gentle thud, and one of the photographs slipped out of her hand again. She bent hastily to retrieve it, straightening to find Blake still staring at her. His mouth was curved into a cold smile that was almost a sneer, and she asked sharply, "Why are you looking at me like that?"

"I'm your husband," he said. "I have the right to look at you any way I choose. I bought that right the day I married you."

"The last time we were together you told me we didn't have a marriage. Only a business deal."

"I've had two days away from you to help me change my mind. Why the hell should I pay all your bills and then have to stand back and watch other men enjoying your body?"

"Peter wasn't enjoying my body," she said. "He was enjoying my *company*. At least he recognizes the fact that I have a mind and a soul, even if you don't."

"Sure, I could see how he was admiring your mind when I walked into the room so unexpectedly. Just what have you and Peter Drake been up to while I've been away?"

"Nothing," she said. "Nothing that would interest you, at any rate. He's been showing me some local places of interest."

"I bet he has! And what did you show him in exchange? Your bed?"

Suddenly her rage flared up to meet his. "What if I did? You've said you don't want me. Why should I condemn myself to a life of chastity just because you don't want me . . ."

"No," Blake said, and she heard the harshness of his indrawn breath. "I've never said I don't want you." With quick, powerful strides he crossed the room and pulled her into his arms. "Why should I pretend when you know damn well I can't be in the same room without wanting to hold you . . . wanting to take you into my bed."

"Two days ago you said you had no desire to make love to me."

His dark eyes glittered as he tightened his hold around her waist. "I don't want *to make love* to you, Kate. What I feel for you at this moment has nothing to do with love."

She twisted her head away, avoiding his angry kisses. "I'm not an object to be picked up whenever you want to have sex. I'm not a thing to be discarded or ignored whenever you feel bored. I'm a woman."

His laugh was harsh with self-mockery. "Do you think I haven't noticed that?" he said huskily. "Do you think any normal man could be shut into a bedroom with you, night after night as I've been, and not go mad with the need to possess you?"

"Your needs give you no right to treat me—" But the rest of her words were never spoken as he tangled his fingers in her hair and jerked her head around to receive his kiss.

She started to resist, but his mouth covered hers in a fury of mingled possession and punishment. She twisted her head, straining to keep her lips away from the ravishment of his mouth. He ignored her resistance, crushing her so close to his body that she could feel both the strength of his hard muscles and the bitter depths of his anger.

"Don't, Blake!" she pleaded. "You've misunderstood— Peter is just a friend. There's no reason for you to behave this way."

"If only it was just because of Peter!" Blake muttered harshly.

"What do you mean?" She wasn't sure she had heard him correctly, but he didn't answer her, and the question died on her lips as his mouth covered hers in another burning kiss. She writhed in his arms, desperate to resist his angry lovemaking but even more desperate to resist the tiny flame of passion that was starting to burn in the pit of her stomach.

He felt her infinitesimal leap of response, even though she tried to disguise it. His touch became less aggressive, and his kisses gradually seduced her with their promise of tender passion. She felt the stiffness leave her body, and she became soft and pliant in his arms.

"No, Blake," she whispered when his hands began to caress her breasts with devastating effect, but she wasn't trying to escape from him any more and they both knew it. She tried to form coherent sentences to tell him to go away from her and never come back, but his lovemaking filled her with passion, leaving no room for rational thought. His caresses seemed to promise her paradise, if she would only surrender. His lips moved softly over her skin, coaxing her into submission, until her whole body shivered with longing. His kisses deepened, drugging her thoughts, so that all she could feel was the heat of her own desire reflected in his body.

She quivered with a strange mixture of fear and triumph as she saw the naked need burning in his eyes.

"Love me, Blake," she murmured. "I want you to love me."

He swore under his breath as he thrust her away from him, pushing unsteady fingers through his hair, then turning aside from her with grim determination. "There can be no talk of love between us," he said. "I refuse to act out any more lies. I want sexual fulfillment and so do you. We're adults. There's no reason to deny our desires. But love doesn't enter into the transaction."

"No—" She whispered an anguished rejection of his words, but her body was already on fire with need. When he kissed her, when his hands cupped her breasts, she made no effort to push him away.

The pressure of his mouth became more urgent, and she was swung off her feet as the room began to revolve around her in a dizzy spiral. She felt the softness of pillows behind her head and realized that Blake had carried her across the room to one of the beds. She made one final effort to turn away from him, to tell him he could not take her while his eyes still blazed with anger and his whole body was rigid with contempt. But his hands ripped her clothes from her, turning her skin to liquid desire wherever they touched. His mouth caressed her, until she was begging him for the ultimate release her body craved.

"I'm your wife, Blake," she whispered in despair as his kisses bruised her lips. "It shouldn't be like this between us."

For a fleeting moment she thought she felt a trace of tenderness in the touch of his mouth, but then passion returned, and she was blind to everything but the intensity of their mutual need.

Afterwards she turned away from him, burying her face in the pillow so he wouldn't see the tears that trickled down her cheeks. For a long time there was silence in the darkened room, then he leaned over and turned her to face him, touching her wet cheeks with fingers that were unexpectedly gentle.

"Don't cry," he said firmly. "I can't stand it when you cry."

She kept her eyes closed, but felt his breath warm against her face, and then the touch of his mouth against her lashes.

"Kate," he said, and she could feel his hand tremble slightly as it stroked her body. "Kate, I want to make love to you."

She opened her eyes, wondering if he understood the significance of his own words. She turned hesitantly into his arms, and he held her close, kissing away the last of her tears.

"Please, Kate," he said. "Make love to me."

It was early when she awoke the next morning, but Blake had already left their room. The rumpled sheets felt cold to her touch, and she pushed them hurriedly away. She showered and dressed with feverish haste, anxious to see Blake again, wishing he had woken her before leaving. She wanted to reassure herself that the tender words he had whispered during the night would still be true in the harsh, clear light of morning.

She hired a cab to take her to the movie location, not caring what Sacha might say about her reappearance on the set. The beach was quieter than it had been on her last visit. There were no stuntmen or extras around, and fewer technicians. Sacha was engrossed in conversation with Joni and Blake. As far as Kate could see, neither Peter Drake nor any of the other major actors were on the set.

She didn't want Sacha to order her away, nor did she want to distract Blake while he was working, so she stood in the shade of a clump of trees, too far from the actors to hear what they were saying unless they shouted. She wondered if it was her overwrought imagination, or if there really was an air of tension hanging over everybody? Sacha, she realized, was not shouting and storming around as he had before, and his air of forced calm increased the impression of strain.

After several minutes of low-voiced instructions, Sacha returned to his seat and gave the signal for the cameras to roll. Blake and Joni stood alone, close to the sea, and it was evident Blake was saying good-bye. He kissed Joni passionately, and she returned his kiss. Kate couldn't hear their murmured exchange of dialogue, but she began to understand the reason for the quiet, almost deserted set when she saw Blake pull Joni into his arms again and kiss her with searing realism. He started to undress her, and Kate instinctively closed her eyes as they sank onto the sand, wrapped in each other's arms.

When she opened her eyes again, Blake and Joni were still locked in a tight clinch, and the movie cameras had moved closer to the couple at the water's edge. She watched, rooted to the spot, as Blake caressed Joni's nearly naked body. When Joni started to remove Blake's shirt, Kate could stand it no longer and turned away, pushing her fist into her mouth to muffle her cry of anguish.

They were actors, she told herself over and over again as she hurried away from the set. She stumbled to a halt in a distant section of the lagoon where she could neither see nor hear the filming. When she'd seen them fighting, the blood hadn't been real, she reminded herself. When they'd fought, the knife blades had been plastic. Why torment herself with thinking that their lovemaking was the real thing?

Because she had no confidence in herself. Because Steven had shattered her pride in herself so that she couldn't think of one good, solid reason why a man like Blake Harrington should love her.

She stared angrily at the placid water of the lagoon and hurled a broken seashell as far out as she could, watching the spreading circle of ripples and wondering if she had the courage to go back to the movie set and talk honestly to Blake.

She walked along the tidewater mark and found a piece of rotten driftwood. She occupied herself by crumbling it into tiny pieces while she tried to gather up the courage to face Blake. When Joni's voice called to her across the sand, she turned around with extreme reluctance.

"Hello, Joni." She looked at the young actress warily, wondering if their meeting was accidental or if Joni had sought her out for some special purpose.

"Hi, Kate." Joni looked more attractive than ever before. She was still wearing the tight pants and strapless top she had worn on the set, but the sophistication of her outfit was contradicted by her mouth, which trembled with a hint of vulnerability that was entirely new. Her eyes looked larger and more brilliant in the makeup she wore. They gleamed, bright and unfathomable, in the sunlight. She looked at Kate for a long, silent moment before her gaze dropped to the pile of broken driftwood at Kate's feet.

"I saw you on the set this morning," she said at last. "What did you think of the scene? It's the culminating point of the movie, you know."

"You were very good," Kate replied stiffly. She rubbed salt into her raw emotions by adding, "I've only seen you twice, but on both occasions I thought your work was outstanding."

"Thanks." Joni didn't reply with any of the flippant remarks Kate had expected. "My part in the movie's over now, but Blake's still working. Sacha has decided to reshoot some of the scenes with Peter Drake. He wants more gritty realism, so he's taken them to the other side of the island, where there's no pretty tropical vegetation." Having given this information, Joni fell silent. In any other woman, Kate would have thought her hesitant manner was caused by embarrassment. With Joni, such an explanation didn't seem possible.

"One day I'm going to be the best actress there is," Joni said when they had both stood in silence for almost a full minute. "Right now, I'm still learning."

"You've always looked very professional to me."

Joni kept her eyes fixed on the pile of driftwood. "When I won the chance to play this part, I was determined to prove I hadn't got it just because I'm Sacha Stein's daughter. There were a lot of angry actresses in Hollywood who were waiting to see me fall on my face, so I threw myself into the character as completely as I could. It was the only way I knew to make her come alive. For the last couple of months I haven't really been Joni Stein. I've been Angel, the girl in the movie."

"Isn't it a bit confusing if you have to change personalities every time you get a new part?"

"Experienced actors don't do what I did," Joni said quietly. "They can separate their performance from their real lives. That's why an actress like Helen Hayes or Vanessa Redgrave is so superb. They're not controlled by their part; they're controlling a character they've consciously created."

"Why are you telling me this, Joni?"

"Blake is a naturally talented performer . . . a born actor, just like I am . . . but he has years of experience behind him. He can separate reality from illusion. When he's acting a scene, for those few minutes he may be the character he's portraying, but when the filming stops, he becomes Blake Harrington again."

Reluctantly, not sure if she was wise to give Joni a glimpse of her private fears, Kate put her doubts into words. "That was a pretty convincing love scene back there for two people who were faking all the emotions."

"Blake was acting," Joni said. "I wasn't." She gave a short, hard laugh. "I don't know why I'm telling you all this. It's like spilling your soul in the confessional. Once you start, you can't stop."

"Are you in love with Blake?"

"I was. I'm not any more, or at any rate, I soon won't be. I'm not interested in eating my heart out for a man who doesn't know I exist." She lifted her gaze from the driftwood and stared at Kate with a touch of defiance. "I guess I have a guilty conscience because I've spent the last month doing my best to wreck your marriage."

"Whatever your plans may have been, you didn't actually do anything to destroy our relationship." With a tinge of bitterness, Kate added, "Blake and I did that to ourselves."

"I helped," Joni said. "When I came to Windhaven Farm, you and Blake seemed so much in love that I went half-crazy with jealousy. You only had to look at each other, and I could feel the airwaves start to sizzle. Worst of all, from my point of view, was the fact that you seemed to be friends. Passionate love affairs can cool off, but friendships are harder to break up, and you two seemed to have the sort of closeness that couples usually get only after they've been married for years and years. I wanted Blake to feel that special closeness for me, but if he couldn't, then I didn't want him to feel that way about anybody."

"You don't have to tell me all this, Joni, you know."

"I'll probably hate myself tomorrow for being dumb enough to admit all this stuff, but I have one more confession to make while I'm feeling in a confessing sort of mood. I wanted to mess up your marriage before it could grow any real roots, so I called the biggest TV station in Milwaukee and told the managing director I was you. I invited him to send a crew to the town hall to cover 'my' wedding."

"You did *what?*"

"I told the TV station when and where you were getting married. If you remember, Blake had already told me what day the ceremony would be. I just had to find out the exact time, and that was easy. I hired an investigator to check the judges' calendars for that particular Friday."

"What in heaven's name did you expect to achieve with all that scheming?"

"Trouble for you," Joni said. "Blake told me you hadn't recognized him, and he forced me to keep my mouth shut about his true identity." She shrugged. "I had nothing to lose by notifying the media, and I guessed you'd be pretty mad at Blake when you found out how he'd deceived you. I thought you might be mad enough to refuse to fly out to Fiji." She shrugged again. "I should have known better. You're such a poised, self-possessed sort of person, I hoped you'd blow your cool right there on camera in front of fifty million viewers. But of course you didn't lose your control for a second. You just smiled that damn, remote smile of yours while Blake stared at you with his heart in his eyes. I hated you more than ever, after I saw that TV news clip."

"If only you could have followed us into our hotel bedroom, you might have been more satisifed," Kate murmured. "Since this seems to be a day for confessions, you may as well know that your plan succeeded beyond your wildest dreams. Not only did you spring your surprise on me, but Blake concluded I'd recognized him from the very beginning and had deliberately set him up. He thinks I married him because he's a very rich and famous man."

"I'm sorry," Joni said simply. "I know I behaved badly. Now that I've finished the movie, I can say that and really mean it. Even so, I wouldn't be giving away all my secrets if I thought there was any chance of taking Blake away from you. Unfortunately, Blake still loves you, Kate. I may as well let you both be happy together, because I'm smart enough to know he'll never turn to me. As far as Blake's concerned, it's you or nobody."

"I wish I was as sure of that as you seem to be."

"I'm leaving Fiji tomorrow, Kate. I wouldn't be going if there was any chance of persuading Blake to look in my direction."

With a defiant toss of her curls, she thrust her chin into the air. "I expect to get nominated for an Oscar for my work on this movie. I'll see you at the awards ceremony, I guess, and I hope to God you're nine months' pregnant and looking terrible."

Kate wanted to resist the unspoken appeal of Joni's brittle apology, but she found it impossible. "I'd like to be pregnant," she said. "And I sincerely hope you get your Oscar."

"Yes, incredible as that seems, you probably do. Like I told you in Wisconsin, you look like the noble type."

"According to you, I can afford to be generous because I have Blake. Good-bye, Joni."

"Good-bye. On second thought, I hope I don't see you at the awards ceremony. With my luck, you'll turn out to be one of those women who drip hormones and look more beautiful when they're pregnant than when they're not."

Joni swung on her heel and walked quickly across the deserted beach. She never once looked back.

Kate left the lagoon more slowly. Blake was still working, so there was no point in hanging around, hoping to speak to him. She walked along the narrow, rutted highway until she came to a small bar with a telephone. She summoned a cab and rode back to the hotel, her mood veering between wild hope and black despair.

The telephone was ringing in her room as she fumbled with her key in the lock. She hurried into the room and snatched up the receiver. Perhaps it was Blake.

"Mrs. Harrington?" asked the operator. "Hold the line, please. We have a call for you from the United States."

The crackle of the cable faded as the connection was made. "Kate? Is that you?"

"Mother?"

"Oh, thank God! I've found you at last. I think I've

called every hotel in Fiji trying to find a Mr. and Mrs. Blake Koehler. You weren't registered anywhere. And even at this hotel, they told me they didn't have anybody by the name of Koehler."

"It was clever of the operator to track me down. We're registered under another name." She didn't give her mother any time to ask awkward questions. "What's the problem, Mother? Everything's all right, I hope?"

"Oh, Kate, it's your father! He's had a stroke and he's in the hospital and he can hardly speak but he keeps asking for you!"

Kate gripped the telephone so tightly that it hurt her fingers. She was only dimly aware of the pain. "I'll be right home," she said. "But Mother, there's only one plane a day out of here, and the journey takes fifteen hours. Tell Dad I'll be there as soon as I can make it."

"Kate!" Even over thousands of miles of Pacific Ocean she could hear the spiraling note of panic in her mother's voice. "Kate, I don't think he's going to pull through! The doctors warned him about it before but he didn't pay any attention. It's his blood pressure . . . And all the worries about the business . . ."

"What do you mean, the doctors warned him? Has he been sick before this?"

"A couple of days after Steven died, he went in for a check-up and Dr. Herschel ordered him to take it easy because his blood pressure was high and his heartbeat irregular. We didn't tell you because we thought you had enough to cope with." Again the hysteria edged into her mother's voice. "Kate, please come home quickly. This time I think he's going to die!"

"He'll be all right, Mother. You know how strong he is." Desperately, Kate searched for words of reassurance to calm her mother, but none seemed to come into her mind. "I'll start making the arrangements right away," she said. "Don't worry, Mother. I'll be there before you know it."

"Yes, I guess it won't seem so bad now that I know

you're on your way home. Thank you, Kate. When I couldn't find you, I was so afraid. . . . Afraid your father wouldn't be able to see you because I had sent you away. . . ."

"Don't think about it," Kate said quickly. "Just get back to Dad and tell him I'm coming home."

"Thank you. Er . . . Kate? . . ."

"Yes?"

"Just thank you, I guess."

When she put down the phone, Kate was surprised to see that there were tiny flecks of blood on the palm of her hand where her nails had dug into the skin. She realized vaguely she was in a state of shock, but the realization wasn't quite sharp enough to pull her back into the harshness of reality. She made the arrangements for her journey in a voice that sounded clear and steady. Her mind, however, was a jumbled haze of anxiety.

All afternoon she tried to contact Blake. She telephoned everybody who might know how to reach him, but without success. Sacha's office simply repeated the facts she had learned from Joni. Blake was working miles off the coast in an unspecified location and could not be contacted.

She gave up in the end and just hoped he would return in time to drive her to the airport. It was strange, she thought as she stuffed clothes into her suitcases, that during the years she had been married to Steven, it had never occurred to her to turn to him for advice or comfort. She had known Blake for such a short time, and their relationship had been fraught with misunderstandings, yet already she felt she needed his strength to support her through this crisis.

She delayed her departure for the airport as long as she could, but Blake, Peter Drake, Sacha, and Joni all remained out of reach. She wrote a note to Blake and left it prominently displayed on his bed. To be doubly sure he knew where she had gone, she left word at the reception desk.

"My father is very ill," she said to the sympathetic receptionist. "My mother needs me at home. Will you be sure that my husband gets the message?"

"Of course," the young woman replied. "I'm so sorry you've had bad news, Mrs. Harrington. Please come back to Fiji soon."

- 12 -

THE JOURNEY BACK to the States was a nightmare of frustration, with every five-minute delay seeming like five hours of waiting. Kate's anxiety was heightened because she had nothing to do except sit in her seat and worry. It was marginally better once the plane landed in Milwaukee, and she could hire a car at the airport for the drive to Forsberg. At least while she was driving she had something to focus on other than grim pictures of her father.

When she finally hurried into her father's room in the intensive care unit of the local hospital, she thought she had arrived too late. Two nurses and a doctor hovered by his bedside, and her mother was weeping silently, the tears coursing down her cheeks unheeded.

"Mother..." Kate whispered, her heart squeezed tight with misery.

"Kate!" her mother exclaimed at once, a smile chasing away her tears. "Kate! Dr. Herschel says your father is going to be fine!" As if overwhelmed by her own good news, she burst out crying again, searching ineffectually for a handkerchief while her body heaved with shuddering sobs.

"Thank heavens!" Kate sighed, and felt her body slump with a mixture of relief and exhaustion. She ran across the shiny tiled floor and folded her arms around her mother, half-expecting to receive a rebuff. To her surprise, her mother leaned against her, resting her head on Kate's shoulders until gradually the convulsive sobbing ceased.

As she cradled her mother in her arms, it struck Kate for the first time how short her mother was. She seemed so frail. A desire to protect her washed over Kate.

The nurses finished whatever task they had been intent upon and moved away from the bed so that Kate could see her father. He looked shrunken, pale, and old, nothing like the powerful, angry man of their last meeting. Plastic tubes stretched from his nose and disappeared down the side of the bed, and his lower arm was almost invisible beneath the cluster of intravenous drips.

"Is he really going to be all right, Dr. Herschel?" she asked, anxiety returning when she saw the clammy grayness of his skin.

"Of course he is," the doctor replied. "Your Dad is a hell of a fighter, Kate, if you'll excuse the language."

Mrs. Forsberg reached behind her for a tissue, and blew her nose firmly, a sign she was once more in control of her emotions.

"So silly of me," she murmured, looking embarrassed as she moved out of her daughter's embrace. "I hope you had a good journey, Kate?" She made an effort to return to her usual polite and impersonal manner.

Kate put her arm gently around her mother's waist, drawing her close, and refusing to slip back into the old formality.

"I had a terrible journey," she said. "But it's all right now that I'm here and know for sure Dad's going to be okay. How long will it be before he recovers completely, Dr. Herschel?"

The doctor pushed his stethoscope further into the pocket of his white coat. He was the family physician and had known Kate since she was in junior high school. "I don't think he is going to recover completely," Dr. Herschel said. "But if he loses some weight and watches his blood pressure—and if he stops trying to do the work of half a dozen normal men—he should be relatively fine. I'll be honest with you, Kate, as I have been with your mother. His left arm is paralyzed, and I don't know if he'll ever regain full use of it."

"Poor Dad!" Kate reached out to touch her father's arm in an instinctive gesture of comfort. "But it could have been so much worse. Why didn't he slow down when you told him to?"

"You know your father, Kate, so I think you know the answer to your own question. I warned him repeatedly and so did your mother. He wouldn't listen to either of us."

"Why didn't you tell me, Mother? It wasn't . . . fair . . . to keep that information from me."

Mrs. Forsberg flushed. "I already told you on the phone. He had the check-up just after Steven . . . You had enough on your hands, what with one thing and another."

"All the time you were comforting me, and helping me with the arrangements for Steven, you were worrying about Dad," Kate said. "And Dad never let on that he wasn't completely well."

"Your mother is a remarkably strong woman, Kate," the doctor interjected. "She absolutely refused to allow you to know the truth, although I warned her that her own health would suffer if she didn't slow down."

"I must have been blind not to guess something was wrong. Dad only visited me a few times but I just assumed he was extra busy in the office."

"I wanted you to think that," her mother said. "You have nothing to reproach yourself for, Kate."

"Well, I have to get back to work," the doctor said after a short silence. "Kate, I'd be happy to see you there and fill you in on all the details of your father's condition. If you'd like to stop by some time tomorrow, call my nurse and see if we can find a half hour when we're both free."

"Thank you, I'd appreciate that."

As soon as Dr. Herschel left, one of the nurses smiled at Kate. "Would you like me to try to find an extra chair for you, Mrs. Harrington? You look tired."

Kate's mother glanced up, surprised. "My daughter's name is Koehler," she said to the nurse. "But it's thoughtful of you to think of finding a chair. She's been traveling all night from Fiji, so she must be exhausted."

Both nurses appeared confused. "I'm sorry, Mrs. Koehler. It's just that I saw pictures of Blake Harrington's wedding on television, and I could have sworn the woman was you." She wrinkled her forehead in obvious puzzlement. "The interviewer said something about Blake Harrington's wife being the daughter of one of Wisconsin's leading industrialists. I really thought it was you."

"It was," Kate said wearily. "It's a long and very complicated story. Do you think my father is likely to regain consciousness soon?"

"Oh, he regained consciousness some time ago," the nurse replied. "He's just sleeping now. I expect he'll be waking up in three or four hours, maybe less."

"Mother . . ." Kate turned uncertainly. "Do you think we could drive back to the house? There's a lot I ought to tell you."

"Yes." Her mother was looking stunned. "But I don't know if I should leave your father," she said.

"We'll telephone you the minute he wakes up," the nurse put in. "You've been here for twenty-four hours without a break, Mrs. Forsberg. I think your daughter's right. You should go home and relax for a couple of hours. I promise you, your husband isn't in any danger."

Reluctantly, Mrs. Forsberg agreed to accompany Kate

back to the house. She was too exhausted, Kate realized, to protest with anything like her usual vigor. Once they were back home, her mother sank onto the sofa, and Kate flopped into the nearest armchair.

"Why did the nurse call you Mrs. Harrington?" her mother asked. "Come to think of it, that's what the hotel receptionist said when I finally reached you in Fiji. 'We don't have a Mr. and Mrs. Blake Koehler, but we have a Mr. and Mrs. Blake Harrington.'" Slowly, Mrs. Forsberg opened her eyes wide and sat up straighter on the sofa. "Blake Harrington!" she breathed. "You're married to Blake *Harrington,* the movie star."

"Well, yes, actually I am."

"Blake Harrington!" her mother repeated. "Of course, I'd have recognized him at once if he hadn't had blue hair in those space movies. I saw *Time Zero,* you know."

"You went to see a movie about outer space?" Kate asked, torn between amusement and surprise. "I know you like going to the movies, but I didn't think space adventure was exactly your thing."

"Nowadays, if you don't go to space adventures or horror shows, there's nothing left to see except dreary movies that are loaded with messages. Even Westerns these days are trying to explain the meaning of life."

"And what's that?" Kate asked, intrigued by this fresh insight into her mother's personality.

"As far as I can discover, the message is that life is thoroughly rotten, and while we're waiting for the final moment of doom, everybody should use a great deal of bad language and have a great deal of strange sex with peculiar people. Monsters from another galaxy seem quite normal in comparison, I assure you." Her mother stopped talking and looked down at her tightly-clenched hands. "Do you really think you can be happy with a movie star, Kate? His background is so . . . different . . . from ours."

"I'm in love with Blake, Mother. I certainly can't be happy without him."

"I wish you'd married Earle Darrin. He would have been such a safe choice for you."

"Marrying somebody you don't love is never safe. I found that out with Steven." Abruptly, Kate rose to her feet. "Mother, could I go and change out of these clothes? I want to be ready to return to the hospital as soon as the nurse calls, and I've been wearing this same outfit since lunchtime yesterday."

"Why don't you take your old room," Mrs. Forsberg suggested politely, accepting her daughter's change of conversation, apparently no more ready than her daughter to press their tenuous intimacy too far. "I'll send the housekeeper up with fresh towels. I'm sure the bed is already made up."

"Thank you," Kate said and escaped to the privacy of her childhood room.

The tubes had been removed from her father's nose when they arrived back at the hospital, and he was propped up on a pile of starched hospital pillows. His face was still so pale that only the darkness of his hair separated the white skin from the white cotton of the pillowcase.

"Hello, Kate. How are you?" His speech was slurred, as if he found his tongue thick and hard to manipulate, and Kate felt a surge of pity. She thought of her father as she had last seen him: charged with energy, restless, a bear of a man always ready to roar with quick impatience. And she prayed silently that he would soon be that way again.

"Hello, Dad." She bent and kissed his cheek gently. "Where are all your nurses? Have you frightened them away already?"

Her father gave a good imitation of a snort. "Silly young thing said I couldn't have a telephone in my room for two weeks. *Two weeks!* Does she know what can happen in the construction industry in two weeks?"

"Jack, you're not to overexcite yourself, or I'll get Dr. Herschel in here," his wife said. "Bill Dexter is in charge temporarily, and he's been with the business for twenty years."

"Bill Dexter!" Mr. Forsberg muttered, his voice still thick and quavering. "What does he know about anything? He wouldn't recognize a problem if he fell over it."

"If he doesn't know anything about the business after twenty years, then you ought to have fired him long ago," Mrs. Forsberg said firmly. "Kate flew home from Fiji especially to see you. She has some...she has some interesting news to tell you about Blake."

Mr. Forsberg frowned. "Blake? What's he got to say for himself? Has he found himself a decent job at last?"

Kate refused to allow herself to get angry. She had spent time during her training with people who were in pain. She recognized that her father needed to appear aggressive in order to cover up his physical weakness and his mental anxiety. "Blake's working hard, Dad. In fact, he's never been unemployed. His professional name is Blake Harrington."

"Who the blazes is Blake Harrington? Was I supposed to jump out of bed with excitement when you told me that?"

"No," Kate replied with a tiny smile. "I'm not at all surprised you don't recognize his name. He's a movie star, Dad. A very famous movie star."

"A movie star! Am I supposed to think that's an improvement over a sensible business man like Earle Darrin? You'd better make sure he settles some money on you while he's got it," her father added irritably. "Otherwise, he'll spend it all on a fleet of pink Rolls Royces, and you'll end up an old woman with no money. You've already given all Steven's inheritance away to that damnfool foundation. You've no more financial sense than a newborn babe, Kate. I don't know what I'm going to do about you."

Quietly, fighting back an angry retort, she laid her hand over his once-strong fingers as they plucked uselessly at the white hospital covers. "You're not going to do anything about me, Dad. I'm a grown-up woman, and I'm responsible for my own life. It's time you stopped worrying about other people and concentrated on making yourself strong again."

"Jack, she's right. This isn't the moment for worrying about Kate's finances."

"Somebody has to think about finances," he said after a slight pause. "Kate's throwing her money away. Giving money to the Center was a waste of good capital that could have been used to provide jobs." Mr. Forsberg spoke forcefully, but his gray complexion showed all too clearly that stubborn will rather than physical strength was keeping him going.

"I still have all that money you put in trust for me when I married Steven," Kate said. "And I want you to take it back, Dad. I know . . . I've heard rumors that Forsberg Industries is having a tough time raising capital with the local banks. Tell them you have my personal funds as security. I know you'll be paying me back with interest as soon as you're fully recovered."

Her father closed his eyes for a moment, and when he opened them again he avoided Kate's gaze. "I don't deserve your generosity," he said. "I tried to force you to sign your trust over to me, just so I could use it as security on my own construction business."

"I see," Kate said after a long pause. "I wish you'd told me the truth when Steven died. The money was yours for the asking, you know. You made it in the first place by your own hard work, so how could I refuse to let you have it back? I'm intelligent enough to understand that the company is trying to ride out a very difficult time in the construction industry."

Her father didn't reply, and Kate looked at him anxiously, although his eyes were still open and he didn't appear to be in worse pain. Her mother answered Kate's questions.

"Your father and I have been accustomed to protecting you, Kate. Perhaps too much. I'm sure it's always hard for parents to realize that their tiny baby has grown into an adult with independent views, but it's twice as hard for parents who have only one child to worry about."

"If only you had been honest with me! If you'd told me the truth about your financial situation, we could have saved each other a great deal of unhappiness."

"I suppose so," Mrs. Forsberg said, her manner still a little stiff. "But I hope our misunderstandings are in the past now. You've married Blake and that's what you wanted, isn't it?"

"Yes," Kate replied, forcing a smile to her lips. She was well aware of the irony of her situation. She had just accused her parents of a lack of honesty in their relationship with her. Now she, in turn, was guilty of the sin of lying by omission. But if her marriage was going to break up, she wouldn't tell her parents her father was on the way to complete recovery. People do very strange things to protect those they love, she thought, as she turned back to speak to her father.

"The offer of my trust funds as security for your company still stands, you know. I guess Bill Dexter could negotiate a loan. Would you trust him to do that, Dad?"

"I would, but it's not necessary," her father said. "A bank in New York approved funds for us at reasonable interest rates a couple of weeks ago. When was it precisely, dear? Can't remember a thing since this damned stroke."

Mrs. Forsberg glanced at Kate and then away again. "It was the day you and Blake got married," she said at last. "Your father and I had an appointment with the president of New York Charter Bank on the day you were to be married. That's why we couldn't come to the ceremony, although of course at the time I couldn't explain to you why it was so important to keep the appointment. At first the president turned us down flat, and your father was pretty much in despair. But he left the bankers a portfolio of facts and figures to go over, and the president must have been favorably impressed. He telephoned us the next morning, just before we were scheduled to fly back to Wisconsin, and said he'd changed his mind. He thought Forsberg Industries deserved the chance to modernize its equipment and make an effort to become competitive in the new, tougher market conditions.

"So your father and I stayed on in New York for two or three days signing the papers, and I suppose that's why we didn't hear anything about your marriage. Our days were pretty full. If we'd seen the TV newscast, I'd have known about Blake being Blake Harrington." Her mother gave Kate a hesitant smile. "But it's all working out, isn't it? Sometimes, just after things look their very worst, everything starts going smoothly again. There's a lot of truth in these old sayings, you know. Your father and I have certainly discovered that it's always darkest just before the dawn."

Kate suddenly realized she felt completely worn out. "I expect you're right, Mother," she said. "Would you mind if I went home and got some sleep? Jet lag seems to be catching up with me." She bent and kissed her father on his cold cheek, touching his good right arm. "Goodnight, Dad, and don't worry about anything. I want to see you up and fighting fit again soon."

She drove home, aching with fatigue, hoping against hope that there would be a message waiting for her from Blake. There was nothing.

She refused to dwell on the possible reasons for Blake's silence and placed a call to him in Fiji. The circuits were all busy, and she had to wait over an hour before the frustrating message came back that Mr. Harrington could not be found in his hotel. She gave the international operator all the other telephone numbers she could think of: Sacha's office, the major hotels, even the number of Joni's suite. Blake still couldn't be found. There was no record of where he was or when he might return.

"Thank you," she said to the operator as she slowly replaced the phone in its cradle. She fiddled with the dials on her radio, trying to find some program that would interest her. She glanced along the rows of children's books left standing on her old bookshelves. It was no use. The unwelcome suspicion still lingered and could not be pushed away. Joni had planned to leave Fiji today. Had Blake left with her?

She crept into bed and drew the covers high around her neck, but she couldn't shut out her dreams. In sleep, her fears came out of their hiding places, and she was forced to spend the night watching the silent movie produced by her subconscious. Over and over again she saw Blake, with Joni's arms wrapped tightly around him, sinking into the softness of the tropical sand. Joni's eyes blazed with a fierce, possessive love. Kate couldn't see Blake's expression.

It was early evening when Kate returned from Dr. Herschel's office, reassured by his concise explanation of the progress her father could expect to make over the next week. Despite this reassurance, she wasn't ready to enter the house and make cheerful conversation with her mother. She wandered into the backyard, and sank onto an ironwork garden chair, scarcely noticing that the metal struck cold against her legs. It was sunny, but there was no warmth in the September air at this late hour of the day. She watched a squirrel chase from tree to tree, its tail fat with the bushiness of autumn growth. It was going to be a cold winter, she thought, then shut her eyes tightly, wondering where she and Blake would be while the squirrel slept away the darkness of winter. She jumped up, startled, when she felt the pale sunlight cut off from her face.

"Blake!" she exclaimed unsteadily, her breath catching in her throat. "Wh-what are you doing here?"

"I'm not willing to let you leave me," he said tersely. "I'm warning you, Kate. I'll use whatever weapons I can think of to keep you with me."

She was shocked by the harshness of his voice. His face was lined with fatigue, his mouth turned down by grim lines of exhaustion. "Leave you?" she repeated. "I don't understand what you mean. I'll only be here for a few days, until my father gets out of the hospital."

Blake's head jerked up sharply. "Is your father in the *hospital?* You mean, he's really sick?"

"He's out of danger now." Kate's voice expressed her bewilderment. "But I told you about Dad in the letter I wrote. And I left a message with the hotel receptionist. Blake . . . I explained it all in the note. Mother and I thought Dad was going to die."

He ran unsteady fingers through his hair, still avoiding Kate's eyes. "The hotel receptionist told me you'd flown home because of a family emergency. Your note only said your father was unwell and your mother needed you at home."

"Well, I'm sorry the receptionist didn't explain more precisely. But why did you think I'd left Fiji if you didn't know Dad had been critically ill? Why have *you* come?"

Blake thrust his hands into his pockets with an abrupt, nervous gesture. "I thought you'd left me," he said curtly. "I thought the family emergency was just a polite fiction, invented for the benefit of the hotel staff."

"But my note . . ."

"Your *note*, Kate, was pretty incoherent. And I guess I was too busy fearing the worst to read it with an open mind." He turned away again, and to Kate's astonishment, she saw a sweep of red darken the pallor of his cheeks. "I can't seem to think too clearly where you're concerned. As soon as your image enters my mind, common sense seems to vanish out the window."

"Are you telling me you flew here because you thought I had left you? Why should you care, Blake? You keep telling me how much you despise me."

"No," he said unsteadily. "I don't despise you. I desire you. I find your body irresistible. I want to . . . make love to you."

"But I don't want your lovemaking," she lied. "You're a conceited devil, aren't you, Blake? Am I supposed to feel flattered because the famous Blake Harrington desires my body?"

"God, you talk too much," he said through clenched teeth. His hands slid beneath her sweater, searching out the warmth of her naked flesh. "I'm not in the mood right now for answering questions."

He bent his head to capture her mouth, but with a muffled cry of protest she pushed his hands away and ran toward the house. He caught up with her easily and pinned her against the sun-warmed brick wall. "Stop fighting the inevitable," he murmured against her mouth. "You know you want me to kiss you."

"No . . ." She gave a tiny, unwilling moan of pleasure as he forced her lips ruthlessly apart with his tongue, while his hands held her body against him with urgent compulsion. She tried to resist the insidious pleasure of his lovemaking, but she felt her body surrendering, and she stiffened, twisting to escape from his arms.

"It's no good, Blake. I won't be *used* this way. Either you agree to try and give our marriage a proper foundation, or I'm leaving you."

"Your body tells me you're a liar, Kate. You won't leave me. You need me as much as I need you, whatever high-sounding platitudes you mouth to conceal it."

"You're an arrogant bastard," she hissed. "And you're wrong about me. I'm not prepared to live with a man who believes I married him for the most sordid motives."

"Right at this moment, I don't care what you've done or why you married me. I only want to hold you . . . to see you naked in bed and watch your eyes turn dark green with passion."

She shut her eyes tightly to block out the pictures his words evoked. She felt his arm move round her, propelling her determinedly inside the house.

"Where are you taking me?" she asked, opening her eyes in a hurry. "Let go of my wrist!"

"Where's your bedroom?"

"That's none of your business! Are you going to add rape to the rest of your humiliating treatment of me?"

He didn't bother to answer as he dragged her up the stairs. "Which room?" he asked tersely. "I'll open every door till I find it. I only want to talk where we won't be interrupted. We'd attracted an audience in the yard, and I didn't think you'd want that."

"An audience?"

"The woman who let me in—the housekeeper—had been observing us for the last ten minutes. She was peeking out through the kitchen curtains."

"We could have talked in the living room," Kate said stiffly. "But since you've dragged me upstairs, this is my bedroom." She opened the door as she spoke and moved as far away from him as the confining space would allow. "What do you want to talk about, Blake?"

"Our marriage. Why you married me..."

"I thought I was in love with you," she admitted with a tight smile. "It seems a long time since I was that naïve."

His face turned pale, and the lines of fatigue seemed to be etched even more sharply than before. "Did you know I was Blake Harrington when you married me, Kate? Tell me the truth...please."

"I had no idea you were Blake Harrington," she said quietly. "I could probably prove that I haven't done any of the things you accuse me of, but I don't want to try. If you can't learn to accept my word, I don't think our marriage will ever be worth anything."

"Then who notified that reporter about our wedding? Who set us up?"

She looked at him steadily. "I didn't, Blake, and if you understood me at all you would know I didn't. Even if you'd told me you were a movie star, it would never have occurred to me to inform a TV station about our marriage. Remember I'm the daughter of a wealthy industrialist. I've been taught to be wary of the media ever since I was a small child."

He glanced up, his expression darkening suddenly. "I've been blind," he said. "It was Joni, wasn't it? That's exactly the sort of stunt she would pull."

Kate expelled her breath in a long sigh. "Yes," she replied. "Joni called the TV station and told the manager she was Kate Danbury. She confessed what she'd done before I left Fiji."

"I can see I owe you an apology," he said. "I've not only been a fool, I've been an arrogant fool. Is it too late for us, Kate?"

She continued to stare out of the window, and he crossed the room in three swift strides. "Look at me, damn you! Is it too late for us to begin again?"

"Are you asking me to continue with our marriage?"

There was a long silence. "Yes," he said at last.

"Because you want to avoid bad publicity?"

"No."

"Because you find my body desirable?"

"That's part of the reason."

"What else, Blake? Why else do you want to be married to me?"

"Because I love you, dammit! Because I can't work, or eat, or sleep, or think, without knowing that you'll be there when I come home. Is that what you want to hear me admit, Kate? Do you want me to grovel some more? I love you, and I can't face the prospect of living without you."

"Is that such a terrible admission?" she asked huskily. "You sound as though you're confessing to first-degree murder."

He made a strange, self-mocking gesture, his shoulders lifting. "I'm not in the habit of leaving myself so vulnerable," he said. "I don't like the feeling."

"But I'm vulnerable, too," she said softly. "I love you, and when you love somebody, they have the power to hurt you as nobody else can."

"Is it true?" he asked. "In spite of everything I've done, you still love me?"

"Yes."

She heard the sharp intake of his breath, but before she could say anything more, he was kissing her passionately, his lips hungry as they moved over her skin. She turned in his arms, running her fingers caressingly along the strong line of his shoulders, and listening to the heavy beat of his heart thudding against her body.

His kiss became so fierce that it bruised her mouth, but she met his passion eagerly, her arms around his neck and her mouth yielding, her desire a match for his. After a long time, his kiss became more gentle, although there was still a raw hunger in the way they clung to each other.

"I want to make love to you," he said urgently. "It seems half a lifetime since I held you in my arms."

She didn't answer him with words, but he must have sensed her willingness. His arm slid under her, and he carried her quickly to the narrow bed. She waited for him to lie down beside her, but instead he sat down on the edge of the bed, lifting her hands to his mouth and pressing a kiss in each palm.

"Tell me again," he said.

She had no need to ask what he meant. "I love you, Blake," she repeated softly. "I'll always love you."

"Never leave me again," he said between kisses. "I thought I would go totally crazy when I came back to the hotel in Fiji and found you were gone."

He stood up from the bed and started to strip off his clothes. She watched him with unconcealed longing, breathless with need by the time he finally joined her on the narrow bed. His fingers were shaking as he unbuttoned her blouse, and she revelled in the knowledge that she had the power to arouse such an intensity of feeling in the man she loved.

He kissed her body as he slowly undressed her, and their passion increased with every touch of his mouth against her skin. There was hunger in his caress, but love and tenderness too, and Kate felt a shaft of intense happiness mingle inextricably with the heat of her desire. Through the darkness of her need, she heard Blake whisper, "I love you, Kate," and then she was blind and deaf to the world around her. Only the fevered hunger Blake unleashed from her body had any reality, and she murmured his name over and over again as he made love to her. When they drifted into sleep, her head resting on his shoulders, their bodies were tangled tightly together on the single bed.

Much later Blake awakened her by switching on a light. She smiled at him, her body still lazy in the aftermath of his loving.

"Somebody has very tactfully slipped a note under our door," Blake said as his hand trailed down the length of her spine. Reluctantly, he got out of bed and padded across to the door. "Your mother is going to spend the evening at the hospital," he said, scanning the note. "She says the house-keeper has left us some dinner in the kitchen."

"Are you hungry?"

"Starving," he said cheerfully. "It seems days since I last had any appetite for food."

When they were dressed and sitting in the kitchen, Blake asked about her father. "Is he going to recover completely, Kate?"

"Except for the partial loss of use of his left hand, the doctor is optimistic," she replied. "And I have some good news about my father's company. A bank in New York has approved a loan on reasonable terms. I'm sure Dad will be able to pull things together now. The corporation just needed a fresh infusion of capital."

"Yes," Blake said abruptly. "I'm sure that was all."

Something in his voice caused Kate to put down her wine glass and confront him with her sudden suspicion. "It was *you*," she said. "*You* called the president of that bank and offered to put up collateral to back Dad's request for a loan."

"Of course I didn't," he said, flushing angrily.

"Oh, Blake! You called on our wedding night, didn't you? Even though you thought I'd tricked you into marriage, you still wanted to help..."

"I don't know how you get these crazy ideas..." But his sheepish expression confirmed her belief.

She paid no attention to his denial and leaned across the

table to touch his hand. "Thank you," she said. "Thank you, Blake."

"I have to let Sacha know where I am," he said, hastily changing the subject. "The poor man is going to have apoplexy if I leave his movie set one more time."

"Yes, you'd better telephone him tonight." Kate could even feel friendly toward Sacha in her present mood. "Do you need to go back to Fiji, Blake?"

"No. We've finished the location work and Sacha is shooting the rest of the movie in California. We'll be able to live in my house. It's on the ocean and has some spectacular views."

"I'll have to look for a new job," Kate said. "Since I do have specialized training, I'd like to use it."

"Fine. I only hope the State of California employs pregnant special education teachers."

"Why? What difference does that make to us?"

"I'm planning to become a father as soon as I can, and I know you'll be thrilled to learn I've selected you as the mother-to-be. . . ."

"Have I already told you you're a conceited devil?" she asked with a husky laugh.

Blake gave her no chance to say anything more. His mouth captured hers, and his kiss made her weak with longing. "Maybe that will persuade you to give the project your full cooperation," he said.

"I need some more persuasion."

"My pleasure, my dear."

It was some time before they heard the sharp rap on the kitchen door. Mrs. Forsberg had already entered the kitchen before Kate could remove herself from Blake's tight embrace.

Her mother's glance fell on the couple entwined on the narrow kitchen chair, and she made a palpable effort to conceal her astonishment. "Er . . . hello, Kate," she said, recovering her poise. "Hello, Blake. I'm pleased to welcome you to Forsberg."

Blake's mouth relaxed into a smile and his arm tightened around Kate's shoulders. "Thank you," he said. "It's certainly a pleasure to be here."

WATCH FOR
6 NEW TITLES EVERY MONTH!

Second Chance at Love™

____ 06318-5 **SAPPHIRE ISLAND #27** Diane Crawford
____ 06335-5 **APHRODITE'S LEGEND #28** Lynn Fairfax
____ 06336-3 **TENDER TRIUMPH #29** Jasmine Craig
____ 06280-4 **AMBER-EYED MAN #30** Johanna Phillips
____ 06249-9 **SUMMER LACE #31** Jenny Nolan
____ 06305-3 **HEARTTHROB #32** Margarett McKean
____ 05626-X **AN ADVERSE ALLIANCE #33** Lucia Curzon
____ 06162-X **LURED INTO DAWN #34** Catherine Mills
____ 06195-6 **SHAMROCK SEASON #35** Jennifer Rose
____ 06304-5 **HOLD FAST TIL MORNING #36** Beth Brookes
____ 06282-0 **HEARTLAND #37** Lynn Fairfax
____ 06408-4 **FROM THIS DAY FORWARD #38** Jolene Adams
____ 05968-4 **THE WIDOW OF BATH #39** Anne Devon

All titles $1.75

WATCH FOR
6 NEW TITLES EVERY MONTH!

Second Chance at Love ™

____ 06400-9 **CACTUS ROSE #40** Zandra Colt

____ 06401-7 **PRIMITIVE SPLENDOR #41** Katherine Swinford

____ 06424-6 **GARDEN OF SILVERY DELIGHTS #42** Sharon Francis

____ 06521-8 **STRANGE POSSESSION #43** Johanna Phillips

____ 06326-6 **CRESCENDO #44** Melinda Harris

____ 05818-1 **INTRIGUING LADY #45** Daphne Woodward

____ 06547-1 **RUNAWAY LOVE #46** Jasmine Craig

____ 06423-8 **BITTERSWEET REVENGE #47** Kelly Adams

____ 06541-2 **STARBURST #48** Tess Ewing

____ 06540-4 **FROM THE TORRID PAST #49** Ann Cristy

____ 06544-7 **RECKLESS LONGING #50** Daisy Logan

____ 05851-3 **LOVE'S MASQUERADE #51** Lillian Marsh

All titles $1.75

QUESTIONNAIRE

1. How many romances do you *read* each month? _____

2. How many of these do you *buy* each month? _____

3. Do you read primarily
   - [ ] novels in romance lines like SECOND CHANCE AT LOVE
   - [ ] historical romances
   - [ ] bestselling contemporary romances
   - [ ] other _____

4. Were the love scenes in this novel (this is book # _____)
   - [ ] too explicit
   - [ ] not explicit enough
   - [ ] tastefully handled

5. On what basis do you make your decision to buy a romance?
   - [ ] friend's recommendation
   - [ ] bookseller's recommendation
   - [ ] art on the front cover
   - [ ] description of the plot on the back cover
   - [ ] author
   - [ ] other _____

6. Where did you buy this book?
   - [ ] chain store (drug, department, etc.)
   - [ ] bookstore
   - [ ] supermarket
   - [ ] other _____

7. Mind telling your age?
   - [ ] under 18
   - [ ] 18 to 30
   - [ ] 31 to 45
   - [ ] over 45

8. How many SECOND CHANCE AT LOVE novels have you read?
   - [ ] this is the first
   - [ ] some (give number, please _____)

9. How do you rate SECOND CHANCE AT LOVE vs. competing lines?
   - [ ] poor
   - [ ] fair
   - [ ] good
   - [ ] excellent

10. Check here if you would like to
   - [ ] receive the SECOND CHANCE AT LOVE Newsletter

• •

Fill-in your name and address below:

name: _____

street address: _____

city _____ state _____ zip _____

Please share your other ideas about romances with us on an additional sheet and attach it securely to this questionnaire.

PLEASE RETURN THIS QUESTIONNAIRE TO:
SECOND CHANCE AT LOVE, THE BERKLEY/JOVE PUBLISHING GROUP
200 Madison Avenue, New York, New York 10016